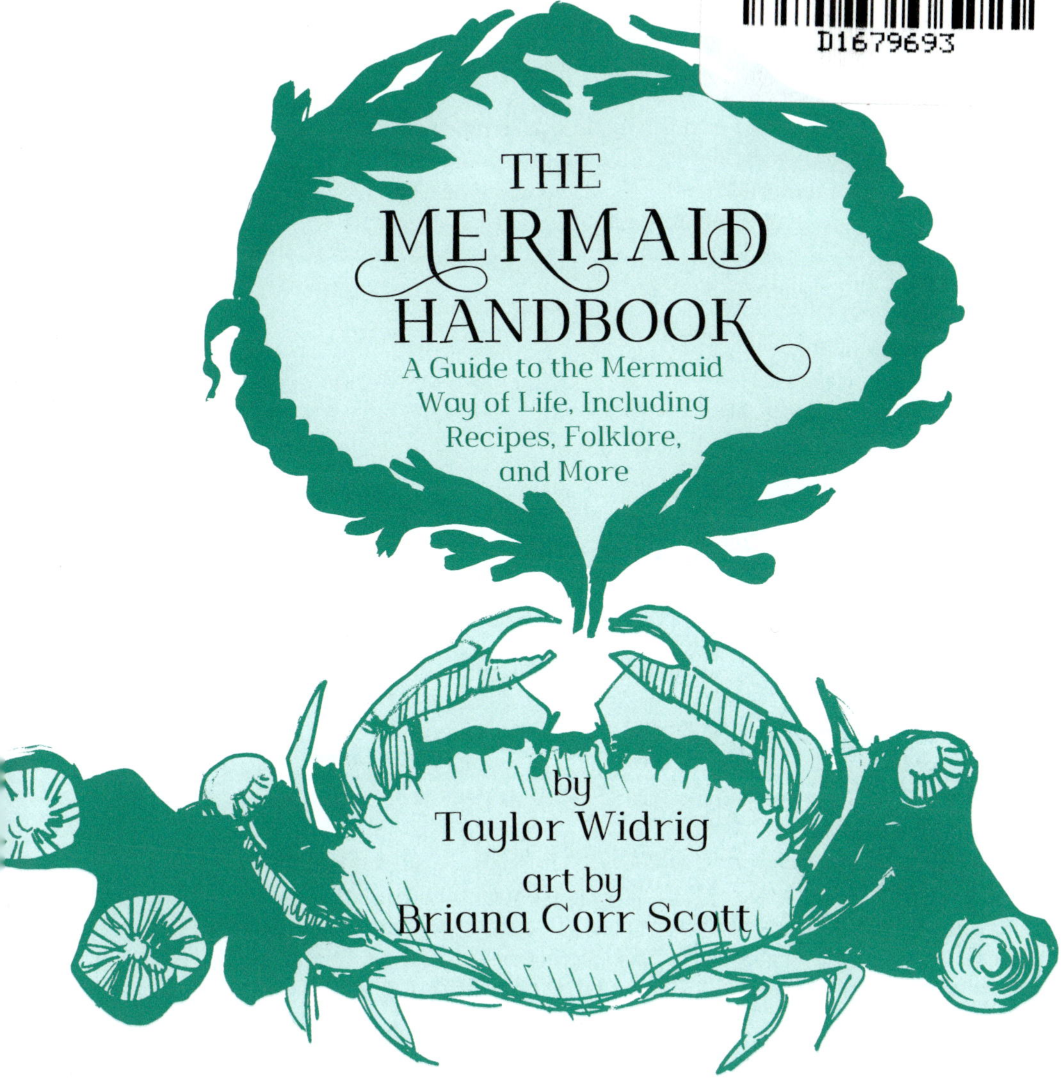

THE MERMAID HANDBOOK

A Guide to the Mermaid Way of Life, Including Recipes, Folklore, and More

by
Taylor Widrig

art by
Briana Corr Scott

Text copyright © 2020, Taylor Widrig
Artwork copyright © 2020, Briana Corr Scott
Introduction to The Seaweed Kingdom © 2020, Dr. Alan Critchley

All rights reserved. No part of this book may be reproduced, stored in a retrieval system or transmitted in any form or by any means without the prior written permission from the publisher, or, in the case of photocopying or other reprographic copying, permission from Access Copyright, 1 Yonge Street, Suite 1900, Toronto, Ontario M5E 1E5.

Nimbus Publishing Limited
3660 Strawberry Hill Street, Halifax, NS, B3K 5A9
(902) 455-4286 nimbus.ca

Printed and bound in Canada
NB1455

Cover design: Heather Bryan
Interior design: Jenn Embree
Editor: Marianne Ward
Editor for the press: Whitney Moran

Library and Archives Canada Cataloguing in Publication

Title: The mermaid handbook : a guide to the mermaid way of life, including recipes, folklore, and more / words by Taylor Widrig ; introduction by Dr. Alan Critchley ; art by Briana Corr Scott.
   Names: Widrig, Taylor, author. | Critchley, Alan T., writer of introduction. | Scott, Briana Corr, 1981- illustrator.
   Identifiers: Canadiana (print) 20200173286 | Canadiana (ebook) 2020018671X | ISBN 9781771088657 (softcover) | ISBN 9781771088664 (HTML)
   Subjects: LCSH: Cooking (Marine algae) | LCSH: Mermaid Fare. | LCSH: Mermaids. | LCSH: Mermaids—Folklore. | LCSH: Mermaids—History. | LCSH: Formulas, recipes, etc.
Classification: LCC TX402 .W53 2020 | DDC 641.6/98—dc23

Nimbus Publishing acknowledges the financial support for its publishing activities from the Government of Canada, the Canada Council for the Arts, and from the Province of Nova Scotia. We are pleased to work in partnership with the Province of Nova Scotia to develop and promote our creative industries for the benefit of all Nova Scotians.

Thank you, Mom,
for your contributions in the creation of this handbook.
Moms know you well.
Like mermaids, they often have mystical powers.

Contents

AUTHOR'S NOTE ... 1

MERMAID FOLKLORE ... 3
- Iara, the Brazilian Mermaid ... 4
- Mami Wata, the African Mermaid ... 7
- Mélusine, the Medieval Mermaid of Albania, France, Germany, and Luxembourg ... 9
- Minnow, the Mi'kmaw Mermaid ... 11
- Ningyo, the Japanese Mermaid ... 13
- Sedna, the Arctic Mermaid ... 15
- Selkies, the Irish/Scottish Mermaids ... 17
- Tabib al-Bahr, Middle Eastern Sea Creature ... 19

THE MERMAID WAY ... 22
- Cultivating Joy ... 23
- Demonstrating Kindness ... 23
- Enjoying Your Ocean Home: Sailing Ships & Beach Trips ... 24
  - Beach Etiquette ... 25
- Protecting Your Ocean Home ... 26
  - Organize Beach Cleanups ... 26
  - Report a Turtle or Cetacean in Danger ... 27
  - Avoid Products that Harm the Ocean ... 27
  - Choose Sustainable Seafood ... 28

Eating Healthy 29
    Health Benefits of Seaweed 30

INTRODUCTION TO THE SEAWEED KINGDOM 33
HISTORICAL USES OF SEAWEED IN THE MARITIMES ... 38
Seaweed and Your Garden 40

COMMON SEA VEGETABLES & HOW TO USE THEM 42
MERMAID RECIPES 47
Snacks and Appetizers 48
    Cranberry Morning Ocean Bars 49
    Energy Balls 51
    Ocean Pâté 52
    Rhubarb and Kelp Bruschetta with Feta Cheese and
    Pickled Red Onion 53
    Sea Pesto 55
    Smoothie Bowls 56

Sushi 101 58
    Shari 59
    Maki Rolls 60
        How to Roll a Maki Roll 61
        Marinated Mushrooms and Cream Cheese Roll 62
        Sweet Potato Panko Roll 63
    Panda Bear Sushi 64
    Sushi Pizza 65

Vietnamese Rice Paper Wraps with Mango or Satay Dipping Sauce 66

Salads 70

Ningyo's Kaiso Seaweed Salad 71

Salad Inspiration and Dressings 72

    Ocean Goddess Dressing 73

    Simply Classic Dressing 74

    Sundried Tomato Dressing 74

    Vegan Caesar Dressing 75

Soups 76

Mexican Gazpacho 77

Miso Soup 78

Pearl Gazpacho 79

Selkies' Seafood Chowder 80

Turmeric Sweet Potato and Carrot Soup with Sautéed Sesame Dulse Swiss Chard 82

Mains 84

Creamy Wakame Casserole Topped with Gomasio 85

DLT – The Famous Dulse, Lettuce, and Tomato Sandwich 87

Kelp Patties 88

Marinated Portobello Mushroom Burgers 90

Mélusine's Sea Crusted Baked Fish with Fiddleheads 92

Salmon Lasagna with White Sauce and Spinach 94

Satay Buckwheat Noodle Bowl with Seared Halibut or Tofu … 96

Thai Mermaid Cakes with Avocado Cream or Sweet Thai Chili Sauce … 98

Sides … 100

Maritime Cauliflower Fried "Rice" … 101

Lemon and Garlic Sautéed Samphire … 102

Mermaid-terranean Cauliflower "Couscous" … 103

Desserts … 106

Carrot Bunny Cake with Ocean Frosting … 107

Mélusine's Classic Mermaid Pie … 109

Micro Fudge Truffles … 111

Raw Chocolate Mousse … 112

Raw Kiwi Coconut Lime Tart … 113

Mermaid Hair and Body … 116

Blonde Hair Rinse … 117

Coconut Sea Hair Mask … 118

Deluxe Whole Leaf Kelp Soak … 119

Fairy Dust for the Bath … 120

Mermaid Bath Salts … 121

For Our Furry Friends … 122

Beach-dog Snacks … 123

Doggy Treats … 125

A MERMAID'S GLOSSARY … 126

Author's Note

LIKE THE OCEAN IN A NOR'EASTER, THIS HANDBOOK CAME about in a perfect swell—tides of legend, history, and recipes to give recognition to my fellow merpeople and their enduring stories, highlight ocean preservation, and celebrate much deserving sea vegetables. As a mermaid, I felt it important to share this information with those on land who are sympathetic with the lives below the sea.

Many foods today for landlubbers, like goji berries and quinoa, are being noted for their "superfood" qualities and admired for the ancient civilizations that grew and ate them. It is my hope that with this handbook, sea vegetables can have their spotlight as one of the oldest superfoods on the planet.

The common desire for most mermaids is to heal, protect, and nourish both body and soul—their own and their loved ones'. By eating a well-balanced, whole-foods diet, including densely nutritious ingredients like sea vegetables, merfolk know they can feel their best and reduce their environmental impact at the same time. Whenever possible, they shop for locally produced ingredients that are seasonally available and avoid certain foods, like seafoods that are not sustainably harvested and antibiotic- and hormone-filled meat, foods that have a negative impact on the Earth's ecosystems and atmosphere.

I hope this book inspires you to tap into your inner mermaid, whether you are above or below the water's surface. Perhaps the diverse and caring merfolk profiled here are your kin. I also hope this book makes you feel good about making lifestyle choices that support the health and well-being not only of yourself, but also of Mother Earth. After all, Mother Earth is a part of each of us, mermaids and humans alike.

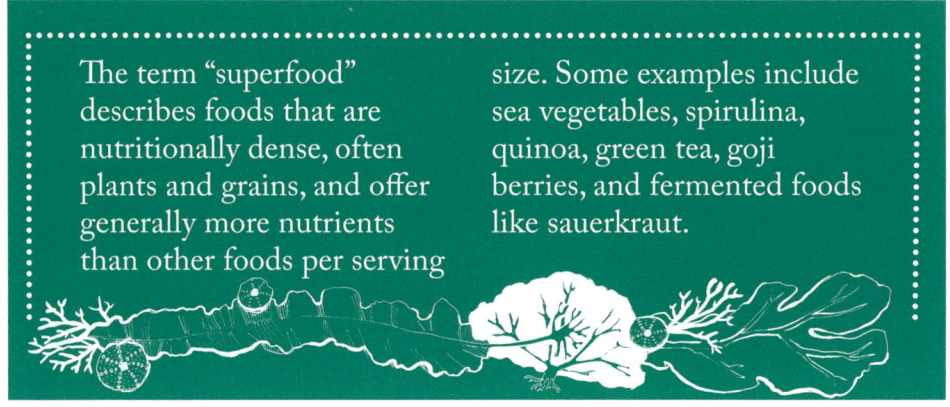

The term "superfood" describes foods that are nutritionally dense, often plants and grains, and offer generally more nutrients than other foods per serving size. Some examples include sea vegetables, spirulina, quinoa, green tea, goji berries, and fermented foods like sauerkraut.

Check the Glossary beginning on page 126 for definitions of the words that appear in **bold** throughout the book.

Mermaid Folklore

WHILE THE ESSENCE OF "MER" (FROM THE FRENCH WORD FOR sea) is a mostly about how you feel, as a mermaid it's important to know who came before you. With that in mind, it's time to get to know some of the many legends of seafolk from around the globe. As a fellow mermaid, I've interpreted these age-old stories for modern-day readers. In general, most legends of merfolk feature significant forces and powers that evoke a sense of magic.

Many of these legends have been passed down for centuries. Who knows what ancient mermaid artifacts might be out there awaiting discovery! In the meantime, let's learn about some of the merpeople from all regions of the globe.

- Iara *4*
- Mami Wata *7*
- Mélusine *9*
- Minnow *11*
- Ningyo *13*
- Sedna *15*
- Selkies *17*
- Tabib al-Bahr *19*

IARA, THE BRAZILIAN MERMAID

Iara is the beautiful, kind river goddess of the Amazon. She once lived as a human in Brazil with her father and two brothers. Her father was a chief healer in the tribe and loved Iara deeply; sometimes it seemed that he loved her more than he loved her two brothers. One night her brothers attempted to harm Iara because they were jealous, and when she fought back the whole community was awakened by the commotion. Iara's father did not believe that it was his sons who started the fight, and he banished Iara to the river where she became a mermaid, maiden of the river.

Iara accepted her fate and became immortal as a warrior mermaid, protecting the waters where she lived and that feed the humans of the region.

Iara's responsibilities were to ensure the safety of those living underneath the surface of the river and to keep an eye on human activities in and around the water. As time passed, Iara became a species; clusters of Iara spread throughout the Amazon and other rivers, streams, and lakes both small and large.

The Amazon River holds many creatures, and Iaras are known to keep a pack of piranhas as pets. They also live with amazingly huge snakes called anacondas and other freshwater snakes and fish that sometimes give Iaras a lift up the river when they have a long journey ahead. The rainforests of Brazil hold plant life that contains natural medicines, and Iaras practice making natural remedies from these plants as well using aquatic plant life for tinctures and other potions.

Iaras love to sing during the daytime. Men can become so enchanted by their beautiful aura and voices that they become dizzy and disoriented, and forget how to get back home.

The goddess Iara is celebrated for her bravery and the strength shown in her decision to make the most of her fate. Iara chose happiness. Her humble personality is obvious in her ability to love all, even those who are acting naughty.

Fun Fact

You may have heard tales of treacherous maidens singing songs to lure ships to the rocky shores, but those are not mermaids—they're sirens.

Underneath her quiet demeanour Iara has great powers, which she uses to bring peace. She never abuses her power, and is always fair and compassionate. All love and respect her because she does not use her power to cause harm.

Iara shows us that the way to overcome darkness is with your inner light, being understanding enough of others' emotions that you can treat them with kindness and compassion, even in times of disharmony. We can also be inspired by her commitment to protecting the rivers.

MAMI WATA, THE AFRICAN MERMAID

Mami Wata, known in many African countries, is a fearless goddess who is loved and revered—no human dares to disobey her. Mami Wata, whose name means "Mother Water," has the ability to shape-shift into a beautiful human woman. Like other water goddesses, she can also cast spells. She has a playful way about her in the tricks that she plays on sailors and other humans, but ultimately Mami Wata encourages goodwill and wants all beings to prosper together.

Mami Wata radiates mysteriousness. She makes occasional appearances in a human body. When she makes her way to urban areas, her bright aura and colourful fashions make her stand out, although she wishes to be discreet. She doesn't want humans to make a big fuss about her.

Mami Wata can be found along the coasts of East and West Africa, as well as Lake Victoria and other lakes throughout the continent. She likes to visit eastern Africa, including Mombosa, Dar es Salaam, and other cities along the coast, and she loves to swim over to the island of Zanzibar for vanilla or downwind to the island of Madagascar to visit the lemurs.

With so many different cultures making up the African continent, Mami Wata is fluent in many languages, including Swahili, Kinyarwanda, Arabic, and French, just to name a few. She has the ability to learn the language of others if she needs to deliver a message.

She walks the shorelines of beaches the day and night, taking captive humans whom she believes hold the ability to create miracles, and when she returns them to the land they have a new outlook on life, which attracts wealth and fame. The humans who return with this powerful, positive, and uplifting outlook on life carry Mami Wata's hope; they deliver the goodwill she wishes to bestow upon humankind.

Mami Wata, like many goddesses and merfolk, loves to use seashell combs to brush her long tresses. You can find her combs on the beach at times washed up on the shoreline. Just as Miami Wata gives humans magical insight, she also has the ability to transform humans into physical water spirits.

This legend of the beautiful African mermaid Mami Wata teaches us that with hard work, and our own special powers, we can accomplish what we set out to do. It is truly powerful to be able to see the opportunities and joy around you and recognize that with them, great change can occur.

MÉLUSINE, THE MEDIEVAL MERMAID OF ALBANIA, FRANCE, GERMANY, AND LUXEMBOURG

Mélusine (also known as Melusina) was from medieval times and has been referenced from western to eastern Europe. The first story about her was written in the late 1300s. Mélusine was one of three daughters born to a fay (an Old English word for fairy) and a king. Her tale illustrates the importance of self-care, and taking time to do the things you enjoy.

One day, while in her human form, Mélusine was discovered at a fountain in the forest by a king. The king fell instantly in love, and he and Mélusine wed. As queen, Mélusine worked to establish peace in the kingdom. Her only request of her husband in exchange for her magical ability to bring him wealth and power was that she have one day a week, Saturday, to herself. Her husband never asked what she got up to on Saturday, but one day his curiosity got the better of him and he peeked through the keyhole of her locked chambers. He saw her in the bathtub and discovered that she was really a mermaid! Unfortunately the king could not keep his promise, and Mélusine was forced to return to the sea.

You can see historical artwork featuring Mélusine in and around fountains throughout Europe. She is often depicted as a maiden with braids and at times showing her full tail. Other times she is shown as a beautiful queen.

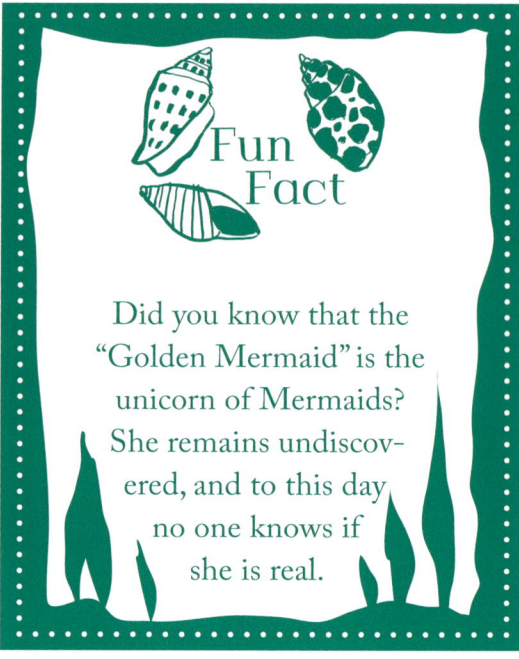

Fun Fact

Did you know that the "Golden Mermaid" is the unicorn of Mermaids? She remains undiscovered, and to this day no one knows if she is real.

Mélusine's request to have Saturdays to herself is similar to the Jewish Shabbat, where no work can be done on Saturdays; it is a day for rest and taking care of your body, spirit, and family. This is sacred time, crucial to your health and your role in all areas of your life, be it school, family, or friendships. You are a team member in all these areas, and the team needs you to be healthy and well rested.

MINNOW, THE MI'KMAW MERMAID

Minnow, a Mi'kmaw mermaid, lived in the waters of eastern Canada and was a brave, loyal spirit. Minnow spent her days weaving baskets of seagrass and kelp to store fish, periwinkles, mussels, oysters, sharks' purses, special land vegetables that grew near the shoreline, and other treasures that she and her finfolk found daily.

Minnow and her people would have swum in and around the Bay of Fundy, which has the highest tides in the world, and up along the South Shore of Nova Scotia past Lunenburg and Chester, the commotion of Halifax, around Cape Breton, and down through the Northumberland Strait. A favourite spot was surely Cape Blomiden, created by the powerful hero Kluskap and located in the Minas Basin at the top of the Bay of Fundy.

Minnow's coastal region was made up of rocky cliffs and sunken caves extending back into the cliffsides, making great homes for many mer-families in the area, as well as deep, coral-filled bays and long, beautiful beaches. Minnow and many other merfolk of her tribe had pet seals and otters, sometimes known to humans as mer-dogs. These cuddly members of the mer-family were able to keep up with the merpeople while they swam around on their daily errands hunting for food.

Like the Mi'kmaq on land, who traditionally carved stone and bones to make day-to-day utensils, Minnow and her merfolk would carve strong pieces of coral and seashells into tools and utensils which they would use to prepare their food within their underwater homes.

Minnow and her kin lived in harmony with the changing seasons: the snowy, cold winters; extra-wet springs (which sound just like rain on top of a tin roof from underneath the sea); bright, warm summer days; and autumn with chilled waters and the potential for hurricanes. Minnow's underwater world was constantly changing.

One day, Minnow and her family encountered some hungry sharks while crossing a bay. Without hesitation, Minnow swam out into the ocean, distracting the sharks away from her loved ones. Acting from the heart, she sacrificed her own life to save her family.

Minnow lived in the spirit of her community, and her own spirit was strong. Like Minnow, your spirit will guide you when you feel in danger or need to make a difficult decision.

NINGYO, THE JAPANESE MERMAID

Records of the Japanese ningyo date back as early as 619 AD in the oldest historical writings of the Nihon Shoki. While many of their mermaid relatives are seen as only half fish, ningyo sometimes appear as a whole fish; other times they appear as part ape and part fish. They surprise unsuspecting onlookers with their scary faces, meant to keep them out of harm's way.

The Pacific Ocean is known for its beautiful pearls, and while it is true that pearls come from oysters and other **bivalve** species, when the ningyo cry, their tears scatter as pearls in the sea. (No one knows how to tell the difference between wild pearls and ningyo tear pearls.)

Ningyo love the cherry blossoms that fall from the trees onto the surface of the water. When they swim to the surface to enjoy the blossoms, they bring their paper umbrellas to protect their skin from the sun.

Ningyo merfolk are highly intuitive, known for their ability to predict catastrophic events. They receive these intuitive messages in their dreams, and use this intuitive knowledge to help protect others.

While ningyo have the ability to give warning of impending natural disasters, like tsunamis, and dangers above, like boats driving recklessly, they are also known to cast spells on those who try to capture them. It is recommended that humans avoid ningyo and leave them in peace unless one chooses to help you. They are known to appear just when you need them.

Fun Fact

Just like the ningyo's tears form pearls in the Pacific Ocean, the tears of mermaids in the Atlantic Ocean form the beach glass that washes up on the shore.

In an ancient reporting of the spells cast by ningyo, a fisherman accidentally trespassed on protected waters to go fishing and was turned into a ningyo. He lived among the ningyo until one day he presented himself to a Japanese prince and told him what had happened. The fisherman ningyo asked the prince if he could be remembered, and the prince made a shrine for the man as a reminder of the value of life. You can visit this ningyo memorial today at the Tenshou-Kyousha Shrine in Fujinomiya, Japan.

Ningyo's message is that we must be grateful for the blessings in our life.

SEDNA, THE ARCTIC MERMAID

The legend of Sedna extends across the Arctic, especially in northern Quebec and Baffin Island, Nunavut. Beautiful, mysterious, ancient sea creatures live in this frozen part of the world near the Arctic Circle, including the "unicorn of the sea," the majestic narwhal.

When Sedna was a human girl, she would go fishing with her family. One day while she was fishing with her father, their kayak met stormy weather. In order to save himself, Sedna's father pushed her overboard. Sedna sank to the ocean bottom and became an all-powerful water spirit. To this day, she is the keeper and caretaker of all the living creatures in the Arctic Ocean realm.

Because of her many responsibilities, Sedna is almost always on the move. She cares for the whales, walruses, fish, seals, and sharks, the humans paddling in their kayaks, the big rabbits that are the same colour as the snow and that come close to the edge of the ice, and the many birds that come to rest there.

Finding feathers is very exciting for Sedna. She believes that feathers are messages from the spirit world, For her, it is like finding the feathers of an angel, letting her know she is on the right path and that she is supported in her efforts.

Sedna also keeps an eye out for polar bears at the surface of the water; they recognize her and are a spirit guide of great importance to her and to many northern coastal Indigenous peoples. Polar bears once taught humans how to hunt for seals, and they symbolize strength, tenacity, and endurance. They teach us to accept our destiny.

Sedna's long, beautiful hair is made of strands of sea kelp and flows with the tides and currents. Fishermen must comb her seaweed hair and bring her presents to keep her happy or she will take away their ability to fish from the sea for food. Her punishment is a reminder that if we do not respect the ocean and its creatures, its blessings will all disappear. Every fisherman knows that he must respect Sedna; they all know that she is loyal to the ocean creatures she protects, and that is why they continue to survive.

Sedna's dedication to protecting the ocean and its inhabitants teaches us to respect what we take from the ocean, that we cannot take too much or without consideration, or it will all disappear.

SELKIES, THE IRISH/SCOTTISH MERMAIDS

Selkies are beautiful creatures with the tail of a seal. They originate from the coastal regions of Ireland and Scotland. Selkies can be seen basking on the rocks in the sunlight; when they remove their sealskins to sunbathe, they are often mistaken for naked humans. Many mermaids reportedly make fantastic wives; as for the Selkie, it is said that it is only when she has taken off her skin—when she is naked and not expecting it—that a man might catch her to be his wife. She can only return to the ocean if she retrieves her sealskin. It is a common tale in Irish and Scottish folklore that many mothers and wives from away were really Selkies in human form, with their seal tail skin hidden in unused chimneys or barns, or buried somewhere on the farm.

Like many other merfolk, Selkies are known to practice magic. Selkies are often referred to as "sea witches" and are known for their ability to perform spells and create miracles, similar to humans who practice paganism and Wicca. The common thread through many legends is the Selkie's connection to the natural world.

The rugged coastal waters of the North Atlantic provide excellent livelihoods for Selkies, with plentiful fish stocks and waves for exercise. You are most likely to be able to spot Selkies in the bays and the mouths of harbours where it is not too rocky, as well as on sand patches or secluded beaches that fishermen pass by at times. While they are in their natural habitat of the ocean, Selkies can be recognized as seals with familiar eyes, often more playful than other seals and with a slightly larger oval shape. They love to relax under the water nestled in a cave with an *Underwater Daily* crossword puzzle; sometimes they even take a nap on the deck of a ship when the crew is sleeping. They love to sunbathe and will sometimes do so in the early morning on wharves at the mouths of bays where ferries pass through so they can play tricks on the watching passengers.

When in their seal form in the water, Selkies bring humans hope through their wonder and playfulness. If their fate brings them to a life on land, Selkies choose to accept this, although they are often caught gazing out at the ocean for extended periods of time. They are very sensitive to everything that goes on around them.

The selkie's story is one of nurturing and commitment to family. Selkies know that there are many different steps to happiness. They keep a lighthearted humour about life and always seem to be in the pursuit of whatever brings them joy. In either form, selkies are mermaids of love, curiosity, caring, and nostalgia for the sea.

TABIB AL-BAHR, MIDDLE EASTERN SEA CREATURE

Tabib al-Bahr is a sea creature of great compassion and is known to be a peacekeeper and a healer. Theirs is a legend of Middle Eastern descent, spanning as far as the Mediterranean. In the Arabic language, "Tabib" means doctor or physician, and "bahr" means "a body of water" (such as a lake, river, or sea), which is why Tabib al-Bahr is called "doctor of the sea." Tabib al-Bahr is neither male nor female. In their forehead is a large yellow gemstone that, when rubbed on the ailing, can miraculously cure illnesses and repair injuries. Tabib al-Bahr is from the warm waters of the Indian Ocean and Persia that hold many treasures of gemstones, gold, and colourful fish. Their body is long, and they are known to be a very fast swimmer.

Accounts of Tabib al-Bahr go as far back as the Abbasid Dynasty, an era that included exploration and research of the oceans and aquatic creatures, similar to the Romantic Era in Europe when people started finding out about forest nymphs and fairies. Artwork established Tabib al-Bahr as an historical figure, not just a tale.

With so much healing and peacekeeping to do, Tabib al-Bahr is rarely bored. They also love to care for themself and can often be found relaxing in the reefs or napping down below in the sandy caves to recharge—especially on weekends. While many humans in the area take hammams (a Turkish bath) or visit saunas to care for their bodies, Tabib al-Bahr has hot sea caves to relax in for a steam. They seem to live to enjoy life and be of service to those in need.

Tabib al-Bahr will not resist capture, instead greeting captors with "shalom aleichem," which is Hebrew for "peace be upon you," or "as-salamu alykum," which is the same message in Arabic. Tabib al-Bahr frees themself with compassion, understanding, and the least resistance. They

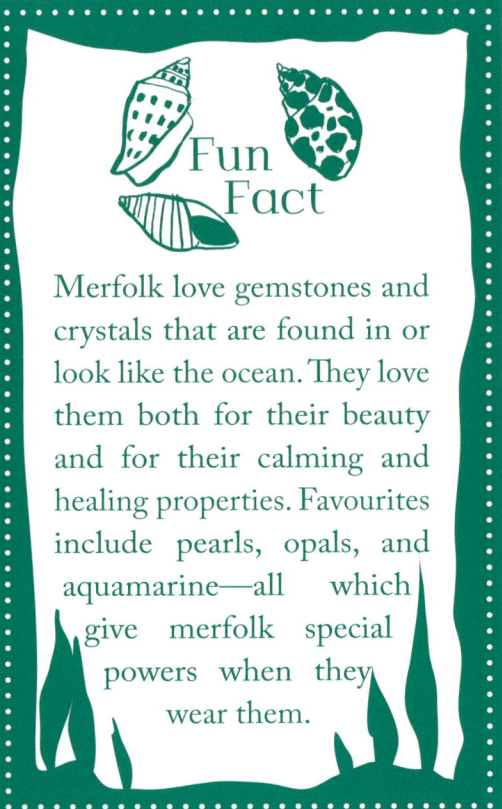

Fun Fact

Merfolk love gemstones and crystals that are found in or look like the ocean. They love them both for their beauty and for their calming and healing properties. Favourites include pearls, opals, and aquamarine—all which give merfolk special powers when they wear them.

show us how to give light in moments of fear and that the light of goodwill always shines through the darkness.

Tabib al-Bahr gives only love, and this is what brings healing to others. This unique creature teaches us to love endlessly and to recognize our own unique abilities so we can use them to be of service.

THE
Mermaid Way

THE WAY OF THE MERMAID IS TO DO THE THINGS THAT BRING you joy. It is in the pursuit of your responsibilities that the magic of your life will happen, and it is the feeling of joy that can guide you in this pursuit, reminding you that you are swimming in the right direction or that where you are is where you should be. There are many opportunities available to you at all times, many choices to make, and mermaids open their eyes to all of the possibilities. They believe that what they want to accomplish is just at the water's surface, and they only need to swim there to reach it.

This section of the book introduces the main personality traits of merfolk—but remember, no two merpeople are the same!

CULTIVATING JOY

Joy can be cultivated by identifying your passions and pursuing those things, and having a lot of fun along the way—like a love of seashell art, seahorse riding, crab racing at school, volunteering at the jellyfish pound, or performing at the coral theatre.

Every merperson in the world was born with a special gift, something that makes them unique. What do you find interesting about yourself? It is in understanding your own gifts and attributes—and in recognizing the gifts and potential in others—that you can determine what you have to offer the world, what will lead you to joy.

It is a great feeling to know that you have a purpose and so does everyone around you. When it is your goal to be a part of something larger than the eyes can see, you can live every day excited about who you are, what you can accomplish, and how much joy there is every step—and splash!—along the way.

DEMONSTRATING KINDNESS

We are all creatures of the sea, each of us a part that makes up one whole. What this means is that we are all like a single drop of water that is part of the whole ocean.

No matter where in the world we live or the colour of our tails, all of us, humans and mermaids alike, want one common thing: peace. Peace to be ourselves, peace to be free, and peace to pursue our life's dreams. When we understand that we are each a small drop of water in the ocean of all living things, we can feel connected compassion. We then put that feeling into action by demonstrating kindness to all the creatures above and below the surface of the water.

ENJOYING YOUR OCEAN HOME: SAILING SHIPS & BEACH TRIPS

Mermaids who find themselves living on land are naturally drawn back to their home in the sea. Many mermaids like to sail, surf, kayak, and participate in other ocean activities.

When up sailing for the day with their sea legs on, mermaids love to bring snacks for their shipmates: fruit, beverages, sandwiches, cheese and crackers, dried seaweed, and tasty baked treats, such as cookies. Mermaids look out for their fellow shipmates and are always keen to lend a helping hand.

Merfolk, like ningyo, are known to be intuitive and can sense the winds and the ocean's swells. It's helpful to have a mermaid on board to let you know where the good wind is and which parts of a harbour to avoid.

Mermaids are playful and mischievous, so whenever one is on board a boat, there is generally a lot of fun involved. While having fun is a part of sailing, it is important to always remember to listen to your captain and be alert while at sea.

BEACH ETIQUETTE

Mermaids on land love nothing more than a day at the beach. You can often spot them doing any of the activities above. They also need to be careful to keep their skin protected and take other precautions to stay safe.

Here is some general beach etiquette to follow:

- Use the buddy system when exploring.
- Don't eat seaweed that is lying on the beach.
- Don't litter on the beach or in the water.
- Be mindful of beachgoers nearby when shaking out your towel.
- Pick up plastic and organize beach cleanups.

PROTECTING YOUR OCEAN HOME

Merfolk understand the importance of keeping their home clean; since their home is the sea, they never ever throw garbage of any kind over the side of a boat. You might think no one is watching, but the mermaids beneath the surface of the ocean will see if you are littering. Our friends down here, like the turtles, can mistake things like plastic bags for food because they look similar to jellyfish, a common meal for many sea creatures. With all that the waters and oceans give to humans, caring for it like your home on land is the best thing to do.

Organize Beach Cleanups

Beach cleanups are a great and simple way to make a contribution to your local coastline and have fun outdoors. Ask your school if they'd like to organize a cleanup activity, or ask your parents to help you search for local groups that organize beach cleanups.

While beach cleanups are important, be sure not to go alone, and when your supervised group does go, dress for the weather and protect your hands and feet. Ensure the trash collected is disposed of or recycled in the proper way, and remember to wash your hands afterwards! We really appreciate it out here in the deep sea, as do all the other creatures who call the ocean their home.

Report a Turtle or Cetacean in Danger

Finding or seeing a sea turtle or cetacean (the scientific name for the group of marine mammals that includes dolphins, whales, and porpoises) in danger is a very serious matter and should be reported immediately. You are advised not to touch the creature, as this could transfer diseases or harm the animal depending on its situation. If you see a dolphin, whale, porpoise, or sea turtle in danger in Canada, report the sighting immediately as instructed on the Department of Fisheries and Oceans website. (Go to dfo-mpo.gc.ca, then search "marine animal incident" and click on the first link.)

Avoid Products that Harm the Ocean

If you live along the coast, do your best to limit household products that contain toxic chemicals, microbeads, or other potentially harmful ingredients. This is because anything that gets washed down the drain in your home has the potential to pollute the ocean. We all know that plastics pollute the ocean and harm sea life. Many companies and families are trying to reduce the use of common plastics. Here are some simple ways to reduce your use of plastic.

- Take your own bags when you go shopping.
- Use reusable cups when you purchase drinks.
- Refuse plastic straws; look for paper straws or bring a reusable one.

- ⭒ Buy foods in bulk to avoid unnecessary packaging and/or shop at zero-waste grocery stores.
- ⭒ Cook at home, eating more natural, whole foods and using fewer processed foods.

Choose Sustainable Seafood

We all know what fishers do—they catch fish and seafood (collectively referred to as "catch") from the ocean and bring it ashore for humans to enjoy. Fishers feed many communities; they are very important humans in the world.

Certain methods of fishing are more sustainable than others; in other words, the fishing methods are in line with systems to protect fish populations (stocks), reduce environmental impact, and prevent disruption in the ecosystem through overfishing. One example of unsustainable fishing is when large amounts of other species ("bycatch") are caught in the pursuit of the primary catch. Depleting stocks of the bycatch can disrupt the

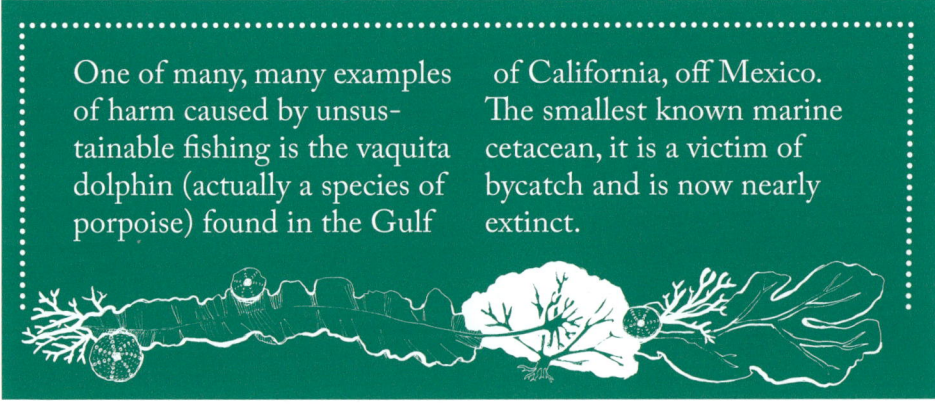

One of many, many examples of harm caused by unsustainable fishing is the vaquita dolphin (actually a species of porpoise) found in the Gulf of California, off Mexico. The smallest known marine cetacean, it is a victim of bycatch and is now nearly extinct.

entire ecosystem. If wild stocks become depleted, it can also be potentially devastating to the local economy. Not only do we need to protect the ocean for the environment, but we need to protect fisheries. This will ensure humans can continue to rely on seafood as a sustainable food source and secure employment for those who depend on the fishery.

Thankfully, there are organizations (for example, MSC Blue Fish Label, Seafood Watch, and Ocean Wise) who use a variety of factors to determine what fish and seafood make it to the sustainable list and what does not. You can visit their websites to learn more on how fish and seafoods are rated through different criteria. Many seafood products available in grocery stores have a small logo on the packaging to let you know it was sustainably sourced. With a little bit of research, you will be prepared to make knowledgeable decisions while shopping at the grocery store and fish market.

EATING HEALTHY

As important as it is to tend to the environment, we also must tend to ourselves, as we know from much of the mermaid lore shared in this book. We can reduce the amount of chemicals and products that pollute our bodies and our planet through the choices we make every day, including our daily diets. By choosing more seasonal and whole foods and fewer processed foods, we can ultimately contribute to a reduction in the manufacturing of food products, such as palm oil or unsustainable seafood, that may have a negative impact on the environment and our ecosystems.

Reducing the consumption of food from animal sources has shown to have a positive effect in reducing carbon emissions. Large-scale farming of animals contributes to greenhouse gas emissions and depletes the nutrients in our soil because of the increased use of land to grow feed for the animals. Choosing a mainly vegetarian or vegan diet has many benefits to humans and mermaids as well as the environment. Ask your parents if this could be an option to try at home.

Health Benefits of Seaweed

Seaweeds offer so many benefits, it is hard to find a place to begin!

We usually use the term "seaweed" to describe these lovely plants of the ocean. When we think of the word "weed," we think of an undesirable pest or a plant that invades our gardens or lawns. It is therefore becoming more common to use the term "sea vegetables" as this is more descriptive of what the plant actually is—a vegetable from the sea.

Sea vegetables offer many nutrients: B vitamins, calcium, fibre, iron, magnesium, protein, probiotics, omega fatty acids, and vitamin C, to name a few. Sea vegetables are also low in calories and carbohydrates. They infuse meals with their nutritional greatness while adding a boost of flavour. Keeping dried seaweeds in the house to use as a vegetable option is perfect for the wintertime when fresh, local vegetables are less available—or if you get snowed in!

When consuming sea vegetables, it is important to note that a little goes a long way. Sea vegetables contain higher amounts of the trace mineral iodine than many other

Fun Fact

Umami, the fifth flavour alongside salty, sweet, sour, and bitter, was first identified in the seaweed kombu by Japanese chemist Kikunae Ikeda at the Tokyo Imperial University in Japan. Umami is the naturally occurring glutamate that makes seaweeds taste so good, more like meat when they are cooked or aged. Its discovery would eventually lead to the manufacturing of monosodium glutamate (MSG), which is an ingredient used to enhance the taste and flavour of foods.

food sources (fish and seafood, dairy products, and some fruit and land vegetables). Iodine is essential for early stage development in children, maternal health, and brain function in adults; iodine deficiency is one of the most common nutritional deficiencies worldwide, which is why most household salt is "iodized." Kelp powder and meal from brown seaweeds (like rockweed or sugar kelp) generally have higher levels of iodine than red species (like Irish moss); they should be sprinkled on top of or in foods and not consumed in quantities over one or two teaspoons per day if raw. (Note that if you are taking medications for the thyroid, you should speak to your doctor prior to consuming seaweeds, which can disrupt these medications due to iodine's role in thyroid activity.)

Because sea vegetables are sources of plant-based protein and iron, they are popular with vegans and vegetarians. The deep, salty, umami-filled flavour of sea vegetables also adds diversity, a meaty taste not commonly found in plant-based protein sources.

As you can see, there are lots of excellent reasons for adding seaweed to your diet. From flavour to nutritional value, sea vegetables offer living organisms—plants, people, and animals—a range of goodness while also being good for the environment. Seaweed provides a nutritionally dense and secure food source for the world's growing population.

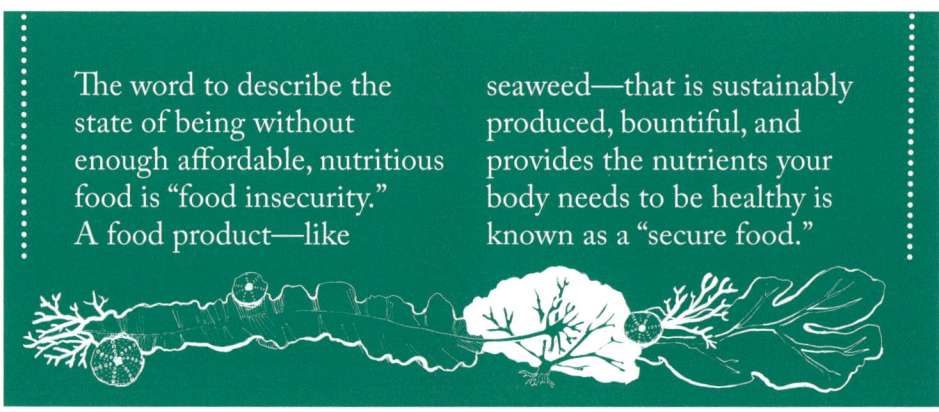

The word to describe the state of being without enough affordable, nutritious food is "food insecurity." A food product—like seaweed—that is sustainably produced, bountiful, and provides the nutrients your body needs to be healthy is known as a "secure food."

AN INTRODUCTION TO
THE Seaweed Kingdom

I THANK THE MERMAID FOR ASKING ME TO WRITE A FEW WORDS on the topic of seaweeds—in all their glory! Now, repeat after me: *All seaweeds are algae, but not all algae are seaweeds.* Algae come in small and large sizes: microalgae are microscopically small, and macroalgae, like seaweeds, are usually large and macroscopic, meaning that you can see them with the naked eye.

According to the Merriam-Webster Dictionary, the not-too-flattering word "seaweed" was first used in 1577. The two words "sea" and "weed" together may make you a little squeamish. Because of this, names such as "sea plants" and "sea veggies" are sometimes used. But we think the word "seaweeds" is a fine way to describe one of nature's greatest resources.

Seaweeds have a long history that dates back to before dinosaurs roamed the Earth. Sadly, though, they did not leave behind many good fossils, because seaweeds don't have hard parts. The fact that seaweeds are still around today just shows how remarkable and resilient they are.

People's use of seaweed can be found in ancient writings. For example, Icelandic sagas, which were written as long ago as the 10th century, refer to the gathering of seaweed, or what they called "sol," for food. That means that the gathering of seaweeds for food has been happening in Iceland for at least the past million years! In ancient Rome, as early as 79 AD, something called "margo," which historians believe is red algae, was gathered and used to fertilize the soil. The monks of Iona, in the Scottish Hebrides, gathered "dulse." Similarly, the Welsh delicacy "laver" has been eaten since at least 1600 AD.

Certain seaweeds were most often used as medicine in ancient Asia. As early as 600 BC some seaweeds were already considered a delicacy, fit for the most honoured guests, including kings. One of these seaweeds is likely to have been "nori." Shipping documents from the 18th century show how Japanese merchants traded raw sugar for konbu (sugar kelp) along the so-called Konbu Road. In China, the first use of seaweed as a food and medicinal ingredient was recorded some 1,700 years ago.

Archaeologists have reported finding the remains of nine seaweed species, from approximately 14,000 years ago, around a fireplace in a human settlement at Monte Verde, Chile. They believe the seaweed was used there as both food and medicine. Research also shows that because seaweeds are so packed with nutrients, they helped with the brain development of the early coastal hominids, the beings that came before humans.

So, what are seaweeds? For convenience, we can call them plants. They **photosynthesize** and capture carbon dioxide. In the process, they release oxygen, just like plants. In fact, long ago all algae, both great and small, worked together to change the Earth's atmosphere, which made it habitable for oxygen-breathing creatures, including us humans!

Algae still contribute greatly to the oxygen in Earth's atmosphere. Globally, algae are more important than land-based forests. Yes, it's true. All algae taken together produce more oxygen for the globe than the Amazon rainforests.

Because light is needed for photosynthesis, seaweeds are found in the coastal waters where enough light shines through. Seaweeds also need certain **pigments** for photosynthesis, especially since the light that reaches them will be less bright the deeper they live in the water. To take advantage of the different amounts of light available, seaweeds come in different colours: red, green, and brown. These colours in seaweed are the result of different combinations of pigments.

In general, seaweeds are "benthic," which means they are attached to a hard sub-layer on the ocean floor. Being attached, seaweeds cannot move from one place to another. They have to be able to withstand their environment—whatever it may bring. For example, at low tide the shoreline on a beach will be exposed. Seaweeds that live in **intertidal zones** are exposed to a lot of light, and because of this they develop their own protective sunscreen! Some even dry out or freeze, depending on the temperature of the air, and produce their own antifreeze. The seaweeds that are attached a little deeper, in the surf zone, must withstand the fast-moving water and lots of wave action. These seaweeds have their own gums and glues, which allow them to stretch and relax and also to hold on to nutrient-rich seawater.

Seaweeds rise to all challenges. Under the right conditions, seaweeds can thrive to provide a marine treasure chest of useful qualities. Because they are dense with nutrients, seaweeds are providing many benefits to other plants, animals, and people all over the world.

There are approximately 10,000 species of seaweeds. Of those species, 6,500 are red algae, 2,000 are brown, and 1,500 are green. That's a lot of diversity. Remember that because nature is always changing, seaweeds are always changing, too. And their characteristics can differ depending on where they are found. If you are planning to collect wild seaweeds, make sure to gather them from safe, clean areas. Also, it is not recommended to collect unattached seaweed from the beach for food, because it could be contaminated. If in doubt, buy seaweeds from a trusted supplier.

Hopefully you now have a better sense of why seaweeds are so amazing, and why they've lasted on Earth for so long. I'd like to end my introduction with a poem by Mary Matilda Howard, who praised seaweeds in her book *Ocean Flowers and Their Teachings* (1846).

> *Oh! Call us not weeds, but flowers of the sea.*
> *For lovely, and gay, and bright-tinted are we!*
> *Our Blush is as deep as the rose of thy bowers.*
> *Then call us not weeds, we are Ocean's gay flowers.*

Dr. Alan Critchley

Historical Uses of Seaweed in the Maritimes

Folks in the Maritimes have snacked on the dried seaweed dulse for centuries. Many Maritimers have fond memories of being made by their parents or grandparents to pick dulse during the summer months and dry it out in the sun or in a woodshed. It was often kept in the house as a nutritious snack or cooking ingredient for things like seafood chowder and clam bakes. Indeed, it is still enjoyed today and is a featured ingredient in the recipe section of this book. But throughout the history of both settlers and Indigenous peoples in the Maritimes, seaweed and marine plants have also had some interesting uses that might surprise you. Let's talk about a few of these uses.

The Mi'kmaq traditionally use eelgrass, a type of seagrass, in weaving baskets. (Seagrass is very important. Scientists look to the health of seagrass to understand the overall health of the ocean.)

If you live in Atlantic Canada, you know how cold it can get in the winter, with the whipping winds and chilly drafts entering through the window panes and woodwork of your home. As a practical solution, people here once used seaweed, a natural, economical, and readily accessible material, to insulate their homes. It made an excellent barrier and provided protection from the cold. There are countless tales of homeowners doing renovations on old houses where dried seaweed, likely rockweed, was found within the walls.

In the 1940s and '50s more processed foods and commercial products were being created, and companies started looking to natural plants that contained "functional ingredients" that they could use in the manufacturing of their products. One of seaweed's big debuts in commercial manufacturing came in the form of carrageenan, a natural **polysaccharide** found in many red seaweed species, including Irish moss, named for the town of Carragheen in Ireland, where the Selkies are from. Carrageenan was being produced on an industrial scale as early as the 1930s for use in

Fun Fact

Starting in the 1930s, Irish moss was harvested largely from Prince Edward Island and sold around the globe as a source of carrageenan. The harvesters were known as "mossers" and often used horse-drawn carts to transport their harvest to where it would be processed and sold.

dairy products such as ice creams and chocolate milk. At one time you had to shake a bottle of chocolate milk so the chocolate at the bottom would spread all throughout the milk, but when manufacturers added carrageenan, it caused the chocolate to become suspended throughout, making it look and taste like chocolate milk without anyone having to shake the bottle.

Another interesting use of carrageenan is in toothpaste, to help it keep its form. That's right, you brush your teeth with a seaweed ingredient (hopefully twice a day)!

SEAWEED AND YOUR GARDEN

Farmer George is a wise man from Newfoundland and a gardener extraordinaire whom I met once on the beach. He promised he wouldn't tell anyone about meeting a mermaid, which made me feel comfortable. He told me all about his gardens and that sea vegetables can be used in your garden, especially if that garden is made of clay or a sandy or acidic soil. The seaweed will give your plants just the right amount of nutrients and minerals they need to thrive.

You can invite family and friends to help you pick dried seaweed off the beach in the autumn to cover your garden beds before the first frost. In spring, after the flower beds awake from their long winter sleep, the snow will melt through the seaweed and the seaweed will disappear into the soil.

Farmer George recommends picking seaweed at the highest and driest point of the shoreline so the sun has had a chance to evaporate most of the salt. Shake off excess sand from the seaweed, bring it back to your garden plot, and mix it into your compost pile. If you do not have a compost pile, you can use the winter blanket method. Please remember that while this collected seaweed is good for your garden, it would not be safe to eat.

We'll explore edible seaweeds in the next section. We mermaids are nurturing beings who lead wholesome lives, which naturally includes eating nutritious food. Seaweeds are vegetables of the sea, and the oceans are mermaids' underwater farms. We know from artwork and numerous legends that mermaids and other merpeople also use sea vegetables as a material for tools and other useful things, like baskets and fashionable headbands. Near the end of the book, you'll even learn how to make mermaid hair and body products and dog treats from seaweed! Seaweed, indeed, is an essential ingredient in the mermaid way of life.

COMMON SEA VEGETABLES & HOW TO USE THEM

The seaweeds in the recipes provided in this book are found in Atlantic Canada, the eastern United States, and Western Europe (including Scandinavia). While we have selected our most treasured species for these recipes, there are many more species of seaweed available, which can also be used in recipes.

Brown Seaweeds

Atlantic Wakame
(Alaria esculenta)

Wakame is famous in the sea vegetable world and is a culinary celebrity for its leading role in miso soup, where it is traditionally used. It can also be ground to use in seasonings, soups, and salad dressings. Atlantic wakame is a different species than the more commonly known species originating from the Pacific but has similar characteristics and grows in Atlantic Canada. Atlantic wakame is similar to sugar kelp but with a deeper, more umami-filled flavour. The texture and flavour make Atlantic wakame very popular, and it is becoming more widely available in North America, either whole leaf or flaked.

In Japan, wakame and konbu (or kombu) are first dried as soon as possible after harvesting and then stored in konbu houses to age the seaweed, which enhances and deepens the umami flavour.

Rockweed
a.k.a. Norweigan kelp, knotted kelp, knotted wrack
(Aschophyllum nodosum)

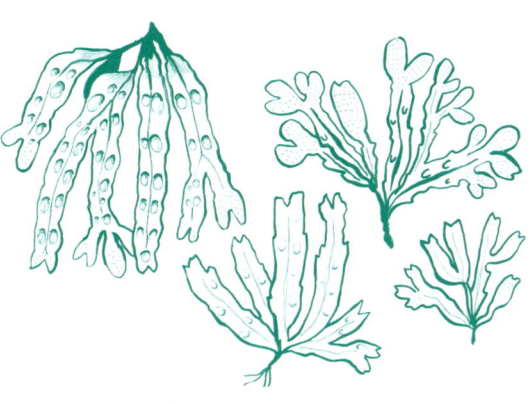

Rockweed is often gold in colour, and can be seen spread across beach rocks. This species is commonly ground into a powder or "meal," which can be added to baked goods like bread or muffins for a boost of nutrients and enhanced texture, or mixed with sea salt for an infused blend to use in soups and salad dressings. The flavour is deep ocean, salty—you can really taste it's seaweed—and most merfolk love this delicious combination.

Sugar Kelp
a.k.a. Atlantic Kombu
(Saccharina latissima)

Sugar kelp grows wild in the ocean and is also cultivated along the eastern and western seaboards of North America and other regions of the world, like Norway. This seaweed is farmed in the ocean, often on lines that look like a mussel farm, and does much of its growing in the springtime. The plant grows in one big blade, and when you dip it in hot water it turns a bright green. Whole, the plant can be blanched (scalded briefly, then drained, cooled in ice water) and cut into noodles for seaweed salad or other cold salad or seafood creations. Dried flakes of sugar kelp can be added to soups and casseroles or sprinkled on avocado toast. Sugar kelp does have a lovely, slightly sweet taste and is a useful ingredient to keep in the kitchen.

Red Seaweeds
Dulse
(*Palmaria palmata*)

Dried dulse is commonly found along the North Atlantic coast of North America, as well as in Europe and Scandinavia. It provides a perfect burst of flavour in many recipes and is a powerhouse of vital nutrients. It can be eaten as a snack right out of the bag or added to savoury cooked dishes like stir-fries or chowder. It can withstand a medium cooking temperature but should be added to dishes near the end of preparation to preserve its soft texture and colour, just like when using fresh herbs. Its flavour is on the fishy spectrum, perfectly salty with an aftertaste of the ocean. Find this species whole leaf or in flaked form in stores, online, or at seasonal farmers' markets.

Irish Moss
a.k.a. Carageen moss
(*Chondrus crispus*)

Irish moss is commonly rehydrated and used as a gelling agent in desserts and jams, meaning it helps the recipe thicken. The compound in Irish moss that lends its jelly gift is carrageenan. Cultivated species—like Hana Tsunomata, known for its beautiful appearance—can be used to make seaweed salad or as a seafood garnish, or they can be mixed in with cooked grains. The product comes dry and is available for mermaids to order online or find at select retailers, maybe even in a seaweed salad mix. Wild Irish moss is packaged dried and whole leaf, which you would then hydrate by soaking or simmering in water to release its carrageenan. Some retailers offer this product bleached white rather than the common pink colour. When eaten in its whole form, Irish moss has a mild ocean flavour.

Now that we know a little bit more about some of mermaids' favourite seaweeds, let's make some delicious food for your next underwater picnic!

Mermaid Recipes

THROUGHOUT THESE RECIPES, YOU MAY come across ingredients that are new to your cupboards. They can generally be found in health- food stores or the natural-food section of most grocery stores. See the glossary beginning on page 126 for a guide to some of the less common ingredients.

❈ Make sure a parent or trusted guardian helps you with these recipes, especially when it comes to using any appliances or sharp utensils.

Snacks AND Appetizers

Mermaids love to keep active, splashing in the water with their seal pets, swimming, and playing hide-and-seek in the coral reefs. Because of their busy lifestyle, they are always hungry!

This section includes some of mermaids' favourite seaside snacks and appetizers.

- Cranberry Morning Ocean Bars *49*
- Energy Balls *51*
- Ocean Pâté *52*
- Rhubarb and Kelp Bruschetta with Feta Cheese and Pickled Red Onions *53*
- Sea Pesto *55*
- Smoothie Bowls *56*

Cranberry Morning Ocean Bars

Makes 1 dozen

Perfect for the lunch box, hiking trip, barbecue, or whenever you want a healthy snack, these granola bars feature cranberries, which are a very special berry to the people living in eastern Canada. Folks in this region go cranberry picking every fall; some even farm cranberries in big bogs. The berry pickers clean and stock their freezers before the snow falls, and the berries last until the following spring, making appearances in sauces, homemade wine, muffins, and other baked goods.

Store these bars in an airtight container for up to 1 week in the refrigerator or in the freezer for up to 3 months.

- 3/4 cup **coconut oil**
- 2 cups cranberries
- 1/4 cup coconut palm sugar
- 2 tbsp maple syrup
- 1 tsp cinnamon
- 1/2 tsp sea salt
- 4 cups oats
- 1 cup sliced almonds
- 1 cup shredded coconut
- 1 tbsp dulse flakes

1. Heat coconut oil in a saucepan over medium heat and add cranberries, sugar, maple syrup, cinnamon, and salt. Bring to a boil then remove from heat, gently mashing the cranberries against the side of the pan.
2. Mix oats, almonds, coconut, and seaweed flakes in a bowl and stir in liquid cranberry mixture.

3. Line a 9 x 13 baking dish with plastic wrap and press the bar mixture into the dish, using more plastic wrap on top to prevent it from sticking to your hands. You can also press it down with a book or smaller pan. The harder you press, the better the bars will turn out!
4. Using a food scraper or knife, cut to form your desired bar size, and refrigerate for a minimum of 1 hour.

Energy Balls

Makes 24 bite-sized balls

These little bites of goodness are perfect for the lunch box, as a dessert, or a snack for any time you're looking for something quick and filling. Two varieties are offered here. For each, combine all ingredients in a food processor and process into a course meal, about 1 minute. Shape into balls of your desired size and store in an airtight container in the fridge. They also freeze well and can be eaten semi-frozen.

Land Lubbers

- 1 cup pitted dates
- 1 cup instant oatmeal
- 1/2 cup chocolate chips
- 1/2 cup shredded coconut
- 1/4 cup dried cranberries (optional)
- 1/4 cup maple syrup
- 2 tsp sugar kelp or dulse flakes

Sweet & Salty

- 3/4 cup pitted dates
- 3/4 cup raisins
- 1/2 cup instant oatmeal
- 1/2 cup toasted sesame seeds
- 1/2 cup tahini
- 1 tbsp sugar kelp or dulse flakes

Ocean Pâté

When we think of pâté we might automatically think of meat and seafood, but here we explore a vegan pâté inspired by the ocean, using dulse for a burst of umami and saltiness.

Sunflower seeds are an excellent source of healthy fats and protein. By soaking them they are activated and the nutrients become more bioavailable, meaning they are more easily absorbed by our bodies. Soaking the seeds also allows the food processor to blend them more smoothly into the perfect base for pâté.

Ocean Pâté goes great in a sandwich, on top of a garden salad, or eaten with crackers and veggies. Store in the fridge for up to 4 days.

- 2 cups sunflower seeds, soaked 4 hours in the fridge, drained, and rinsed
- 1/2 cup water
- 1/2 cup fresh parsley, chopped
- 1/3 cup celery, minced
- 1/3 cup lemon juice
- 1/3 cup red onion, minced
- 3-4 tbsp dulse flakes (depending on how seafood-y you like it!)
- 2 tbsp fresh dill, chopped
- 1 tsp sea salt

1. Combine sunflower seeds and water in a food processor and process for about 2 minutes or until it forms a paste.
2. Add remaining ingredients and process until smooth.

Rhubarb and Kelp Bruschetta with Feta Cheese and Pickled Red Onion

Makes about 24 pieces

It's safe to call rhubarb a Maritime treasure, with its most common uses being crisps, crumbles, pies, and jams. Many a rhubarb plant is plundered during the summer months by grandmothers, neighbours, and anyone with a garden.

This recipe puts a Maritime twist on traditional Italian bruschetta, using rhubarb instead of tomatoes for the acidic flavour. The balsamic vinegar reduction used to finish the bruschetta can be found at many grocery stores in the condiment or international aisle.

- 1 baguette, sliced in 1/4-inch pieces
- 4 medium stalks rhubarb, cut, boiled until tender, and slightly mashed
- 3 tbsp olive oil
- 1 tbsp Atlantic wakame or dulse flakes
- 2 tsp balsamic vinegar
- 1 tsp maple syrup
- salt and pepper, to taste
- 1/2 cup crumbled feta cheese
- 1/2 cup pickled red onion
- balsamic vinegar reduction

1. Preheat oven to 400°F. Line a baking sheet with parchment paper, lay the sliced baguette in rows on the sheet, and toast for 4 minutes or until browned.

MERMAID RECIPES

2. In a medium bowl, mix cooked rhubarb, oil, sugar kelp flakes, balsamic vinegar, and maple syrup. Season with salt and pepper.
3. Spoon rhubarb mixture over baguette slices and sprinkle with crumbled feta cheese. Bake until browned on top, 8–10 minutes.
4. Arrange on a serving platter and top with pickled red onion. Drizzle with balsamic reduction for a taste of sweet.

Sea Pesto

Perfect for any occasion, this nutritious, raw, vegan pesto is a great way to eat more greens and can be used as a spread on baguette, in sandwiches, or as a pasta sauce when mixed with olive oil. Traditional pesto uses cheese; here we use nutritional yeast instead. Store in an airtight container in the fridge.

- 4 cups broccoli florets
- 1 cup basil
- 1/2 cup pine nuts
- 3 tbsp sugar kelp or dulse flakes
- 2 garlic cloves
- juice of 1/2 a lemon
- 1 tsp salt
- 3/4 cup olive oil
- 1/4 cup nutritional yeast

1. Place broccoli florets in a food processor and pulse gently.
2. Add all remaining ingredients except oil and yeast. Process as you drizzle in oil until the mixture has become a smooth paste.
3. Stir in nutritional yeast.

MERMAID RECIPES

Smoothie Bowls

Serves 1 or 2

Smoothie bowls are all the rage, and one might ask, how are they different than a regular smoothie? The answer is that they have more of an ice cream texture, which is achieved by using more frozen banana and other frozen fruits. Eating your smoothie in the form of ice cream is always fun. You might actually stop craving real dairy ice cream, because nothing tastes as sweet and delicious as pure fruit. The best frozen fruits to use are those with low water content and that are less seedy (like banana, cherry, mango, pineapple, and strawberry). You could store the smoothie in the refrigerator or freezer, but chances are it will be gone in an evening just like a traditional pint of dairy ice cream.

Below are some suggested combinations. Feel free to experiment and create your own!

- **Chocolate:** 4 frozen bananas, 1/4 cup cocoa, 3 tbsp maple syrup
- **Cherry:** 4 cups frozen cherries, juice of 1/2 a lemon, 1 tbsp maple syrup
- **Strawberry Banana:** 2 frozen bananas, 2 cups frozen strawberries, juice of 1/2 a lemon, 3 tbsp water
- **Mango Lime:** 4 cups frozen mango, juice of 1 lime, 1 tbsp maple syrup

1. Add all ingredients to a food processor or high-speed blender and process until smooth. The colour will change and become slightly lighter as the fruit fully blends. If the fruit is rock hard and you need some liquid to get it going, add up to 3 tbsp warm water.
2. Pour into a bowl and, if desired, top with sliced almonds, cashews, chocolate nibs, shaved coconut, ground flax seed, dried fruit, hemp hearts, lemon or lime zest, pumpkin or sunflower seeds, or whole berries.

Sushi 101

Japanese cuisine is known to have some of the highest standards for top-quality fresh ingredients and skillfully combined flavours—it is often an art form. Remember that it was the Japanese who discovered and named umami, the fifth taste, and that seaweed was the original source of umami! Various seaweeds are commonly found in Japanese cuisine, including sushi.

Sushi, in fact, is the primary way the Western world has come to know and consume seaweed. Sushi is a favourite for many all over the world (and under the sea!). The use of accompanying pickled ginger and wasabi paste creates many different flavours in each bite.

This section includes some of the sushi recipes most beloved by mermaids everywhere.

- Shari *59*
- Maki Rolls *60*
  - How to Roll a Maki Roll *61*
  - Marinated Mushrooms and Cream Cheese Roll *62*
  - Sweet Potato Panko Roll *63*
- Panda Bear Sushi *64*
- Sushi Pizza *65*
- Vietnamese Rice Paper Wraps with Mango or Satay Dipping Sauce *66*

Shari

Makes approximately 5 cups

Sushi rice (called shari in Japan) is different from other rice varieties in that it is very starchy and glutinous, which allows it to have a "sticky" texture when cooked. The rice is traditionally cooked in a bamboo steamer over a pot of boiling water and then seasoned with sweetened rice vinegar.

- 2 cups short grain Japanese rice
- 1/4 cup **rice vinegar**
- 1 tbsp sugar
- 2 tsp salt
- 2 cups water

1. Place rice in a fine mesh strainer and rinse until the water runs clear, about 2 minutes. Set over a bowl to drain while you prepare your seasoning.
2. Combine vinegar, sugar, and salt in a saucepan over medium heat and whisk together until sugar and salt have dissolved. Set aside to cool.
3. Using a medium saucepan with a tight fitting lid, combine equal parts rice and cold water and bring to a boil over high heat. Cover and cook over medium heat for 10 minutes. Reduce the heat to low and cook for 10 minutes longer. Remove from the heat and let stand, covered, for 15 minutes. (Alternatively, use a rice cooker.)
4. Transfer rice into large mixing bowl and sprinkle half of the seasoned vinegar over the rice. Mix well then add remaining seasoning to taste. Let cool for 20 minutes before making sushi rolls.

Maki Rolls

Also known as nori maki, these rolls can include a variety of different fillings. Maki uses flat nori seaweed sheets, and are the vegetarian version of traditional sushi, which features raw fish and seafood. Maki rolls make a great grab-and-go lunch and can be eaten as a snack any time. In addition to the recipes on the next two pages, here are just a few more ideas for fillings:

- carrot, cucumber, and avocado
- pickled cucumber and ginger
- seasoned tofu
- tempura vegetables

Use your imagination and have fun!

If you would like to enjoy eating mermaid maki and sushi without the glutinous rice grain, you can prepare grated cauliflower rice or use quinoa as a substitute. Be aware, though, that rolls made with these substitutes will not stick together as well.

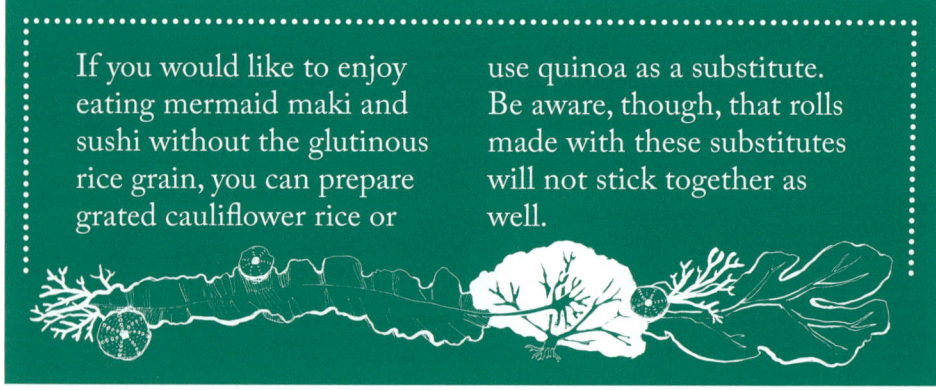

How to Roll a Maki Roll

- ✯ Prepare your rolling station and have these things ready: a bowl of cool water, shari rice, fillings, a dry tea towel, your bamboo rolling mat, nori seaweed sheets, measuring cups, and a plate or platter to place the finished rolls on.
- ✯ Begin one roll at a time: first, place seaweed sheet in line with the bottom of the rolling mat (end closest to you).
- ✯ Wet your fingers and scoop 1/3 cup prepared shari and arrange over the seaweed sheet, starting from about 1 inch from the bottom.
- ✯ Arrange your fillings on the rice in a line, going from one side to the other, beginning where the rice starts on the seaweed sheet.
- ✯ Very firmly begin to press the roll upwards, rolling the bamboo up and over, until you reach the end of the rice.
- ✯ To seal the roll, press the part of the seaweed sheet that was at the bottom before rolling to close the roll and wet it with your fingers if it is too dry.
- ✯ Place roll seam-side-down on a platter.
- ✯ Complete the remainder of rolls and refrigerate for 20 minutes before slicing.
- ✯ Prepare your sushi platters and table with wasabi paste, soy sauce, pickled ginger, and maybe seaweed salad!
- ✯ Place the rolls seam-side-down on a cutting board, and with supervision slice the sushi into 1/2- or 1-inch-thick pieces, depending on desired size. Enjoy!

Marinated Mushrooms and Cream Cheese Roll

Makes 6 rolls

The ultimate vegetarian umami Maki experience, using marinated mushrooms and cream cheese for a deep flavoured, savory roll.

- 4 brown cremini or mini portobello mushrooms, sliced
- 1/4 cup **tamari** soy sauce
- 2 cups steamed shari
- 6 sheets of nori seaweed paper
- 1/4 cup cream cheese, softened

1. Soak the mushroom slices in the tamari while you are preparing the roll, or as long as overnight in the fridge.
2. Spread rice evenly over the nori paper.
3. Spread cream cheese across the centre and top with the marinated mushrooms.
4. Roll, slice, and enjoy.

Sweet Potato Panko Roll

Makes 6 rolls

Panko is basically Japan's version of bread crumbs. It adds a crunch to sushi rolls and is used in tempura batter.

- 2 cups steamed shari
- 6 sheets of nori seaweed paper
- 3/4 cup panko
- 1 sweet potato, peeled, roasted or boiled, and cut into 1/2-inch cubes or strips

1. Spread rice evenly over the nori wraps up to 1 inch from the top, leaving a space to seal the roll and so that it will close easily.
2. Sprinkle just enough panko to coat the rice.
3. Lay the prepared sweet potato across the centre.
4. Roll tightly and enjoy.

MERMAID RECIPES

Panda Bear Sushi

Makes about 8 pandas

Creating highly adorable panda bears out of sushi rice and nori sheet seaweed might be the perfect way to let someone know you love them. These sushi bears are sure to put smiles on faces and are also very practical for the lunch box and snacks on the go. The panda bear rice balls, or any rice balls, are best stored in an airtight container or wrapped in plastic wrap.

- 2 sheets nori seaweed paper (+1 extra just in case)
- 2 cups shari

1. Use scissors* to cut each seaweed sheet into the shapes needed to create a panda bear: oval eye patches, rounded ears, four paws, a nose, a mouth—maybe even a tuxedo. Set pieces aside.
2. Dampen your hands with cold water to prevent the rice from sticking to them as you work. Form 1/4 cup prepared sushi rice into an oval ball. (For smaller pandas, use 2 tbsp.)
3. Place the nori pieces on the rice ball to create your sushi panda and surprise your lucky luncher.

*Please note: it is best to cut out the panda pieces before handling the rice, as you do not want to get the sushi sheets wet before cutting with scissors.

Sushi Pizza

Sushi Pizza is a popular North American trend popular combining two favourite things: sushi and pizza! The sushi rice is shaped like a round pizza and often coated in panko before deep-frying, then adding desired toppings, and drizzling with sauces before serving.

- 1 cup shari
- panko bread crumbs (optional)
- 1/2 avocado, sliced
- grilled tofu, crab, or smoked salmon
- **hoisin**, Sweet Thai Chili Sauce, or Creamy Wasabi

1. Shape shari into a pizza-like disc on a serving plate. If you want to take it to the next level, coat the shari pizza in panko and deep-fry it.
2. Top with sliced avocado and grilled tofu or seafood, then drizzle it with hoisin sauce, Sweet Thai Chili Sauce (see recipe for Thai Mermaid Cakes on page 96), or Creamy Wasabi (2 tsp wasabi powder, 3 tbsp mayonnaise, and a pinch of salt).

Vietnamese Rice Paper Wraps with Mango or Satay Dipping Sauce

Makes 1 dozen

These rice paper wraps are always a winner and come in handy for quick lunches, appetizers, and party platters. They can be made using a variety of ingredients, but the common champions are listed below. When paired with Mango Dipping Sauce and seaweed salad, Vietnamese Rice Paper Wraps create a "spa cuisine" lunch, suitable for sea goddesses and merpeople. These wraps are also delicious with **Satay Dipping Sauce** or many humans' favourite, Sweet Thai Chili Sauce (see page 99).

- 2 stalks celery
- 2 green onions, sliced thin
- 1 medium carrot, peeled
- 1 cucumber
- 1 avocado, halved
- 6 rice paper wraps
- 6 romaine leaves, cut to make a 4-inch long leaf lengthwise
- 1 handful of cilantro, basil, and mint chopped roughly and mixed together

1. Cut the ends off of the celery, green onions, carrot, and cucumber and then cut them to make them 4 inches long.
2. Practice your knife skills by cutting celery, carrot, cucumber, and avocado in half lengthwise and then into 1/4-inch julienned strips.

Alternatively, you can use a julienne peeler or mandolin. (Ask your parents for help with this step.)

3. Arrange prepared ingredients on a platter for easy assembly.
4. Fill a large bowl with warm water and, working with two wraps at a time, dip each wrap in the water, ensuring they get completely wet. Shake off water and lay flat on a clean cutting board.
5. Place 1 romaine leaf across the wrap about 1 inch from the bottom and add celery, carrot, cucumber, and green onion lengthwise inside the romaine. Sprinkle the herbs on top and add avocado.
6. Keeping the rice paper wrap tight against the veggies, start to roll upwards. When you have reached 3/4 of the way, fold the ends inwards and seal at the top. It is very important to keep the contents tight so the wraps won't fall apart when you cut them.
7. Cut the rolled wraps in half on a diagonal to expose their pretty contents.

Mango Dipping Sauce

To create this spectacular Mango Dipping Sauce, add all ingredients in a high-speed blender and blend until completely smooth, about 2 minutes. Stays fresh for up to 3 days in the refrigerator in an airtight container.

- 1 mango, peeled, core removed, and chopped
- 1/2 cup chopped pineapple
- juice of 1 lemon
- 1/4 cup red onion, minced
- 1-inch piece ginger
- 1 Thai chili
- 1 garlic clove
- 1 tsp pink Himalayan salt

Satay Dipping Sauce

This Satay Dipping Sauce can be enjoyed cold or warm, but I think it's better a little bit warm. For the cold version, place all ingredients in a high-speed blender and blend until smooth, about 1 minute. The sauce will thicken once it's refrigerated. For a warm dipping sauce, whisk all ingredients together in a small saucepan over medium heat until it starts to bubble. Serve immediately.

- 1/2 cup peanut or almond butter
- 1/4 cup soy sauce
- 1 tbsp honey or maple syrup
- 1 tbsp **rice vinegar**
- 1 tbsp **sesame oil**
- sriracha or hot sauce (optional)

Salads

Salads are known far and wide, and provide the body with often raw, nutrient-packed vegetables and superfoods. Homemade salad dressings are simple to make and can provide additional nutrients to your salads if made with quality and sustainable oils, flax meal, and natural garlic and ginger.

Salads come in many forms, from the garden salad to seaweed salad, grain salad or potato—eating salad is a lifelong thing, whether you're living on land or in the sea.

- ☆ Ningyo's Kaiso Seaweed Salad 71
- ☆ Salad Inspiration & Dressings 72
  - ❀ Ocean Goddess 73
  - ❀ Simply Classic 74
  - ❀ Sundried Tomato 74
  - ❀ Vegan Caesar 75

Ningyo's Kaiso Seaweed Salad

Serves 2–4

You will commonly find seaweed salad in sushi restaurants. It is traditionally made with blanched and sliced young kombu and wakame seaweed varieties. Kaiso Seaweed Salad has been enjoyed by many on land and sea. The Hana Tsunomata seaweed, a cultivated variety, boasts 40 percent of your recommended daily iron per serving—perfect for the vegetarian mermaid.

This is a great salad to accompany sushi platters or in individual bowls. A much-loved way to eat this salad is atop steamed rice sprinkled with Gomasio seasoning, or mixed in with cooked buckwheat noodles. It can also be used as a garnish on top of seafood canapés and hors doeuvres, or alongside seared seafood or tofu. Stays fresh up to 1 week in the refrigerator and freezes well.

- 1 cup dried cultivated Irish moss (Hana Tsunomata)
- 1 tbsp dulse or Atlantic wakame flakes (optional)
- 2 tbsp gluten-free **tamari** soy sauce
- 1 tbsp maple syrup
- 1 tbsp **rice vinegar**
- 2 tsp **sesame oil**
- 1/4 cup toasted sesame seeds

1. Rehydrate (soak) seaweed in room temperature water for 8 minutes. Drain and shake or pat dry to remove excess water.
2. Whisk together wet ingredients, pour over seaweed, and mix well. Stir in toasted sesame seeds. Marinate for a minimum of 20 minutes before serving.

Salad Inspiration & Dressings

There are so many options to choose from for salads that can be embraced and enjoyed every day. Homemade salad dressings are a great way to jazz up greens while adding protein and other nutrients from nuts, seeds, supplement powders, and oils. Alternatively, you can eat your greens with simple but tasty olive oil and lemon juice, with salt and pepper to taste. We mermaids love sel de mer (a.k.a. sea salt), of course.

Eating veggies in season makes shopping for them even more exciting because there will always be something new. Purchasing local, in-season, fresh veggies not only adds diversity to the diet but it is better for the environment, because it reduces the carbon (CO_2) emissions from shipping.

Mermaids' Favourite Salad Greens & Veggie Options:

arugula, cabbage, lettuce (Boston, leaf lettuce, romaine, etc.), spinach, Swiss chard, and watercress, to name just a few. Look for what is in season and toss in other colourful vegetables (for example, peppers, tomatoes, radish) and ingredients like nuts, seeds, or olives.

Mermaids' Choice Dressings

The Simply Classic uses the Mason jar method. The other three dressings are made by blending all ingredients in a high-speed blender or food processor.

Ocean Goddess Dressing

- 1 cup raw cashews, soaked for two hours and drained
- 3 dates
- 3 garlic cloves
- 2 tbsp chopped fresh Italian parsley
- 2 tbsp chopped green onions
- 1 tbsp minced red onion
- juice of 1 lemon
- 2 tsp dried dill
- 2 tsp onion powder
- 1 tsp **Herbamare**, Herbed Low-Sodium Seasoning (see sidebar below), pink Himalayan salt, or sea salt

Herbed Low-Sodium Seasoning

- 1/2 cup sea salt
- 1 tsp celery seeds
- 1 tsp dried basil
- 1 tsp dried dill
- 1 tsp dried oregano
- 1 tsp dried parsley
- 1 tsp dried rosemary
- 1 tsp dried sage
- 1 tsp dried thyme
- 1 tsp garlic powder
- 1 tsp onion powder
- 1 tsp sugar kelp, dulse, or Atlantic wakame flakes

Place all ingredients in a food processor or high-speed blender and process for about 30 seconds or until all herbs and salt are approximately the same size. Store in a Mason jar or airtight container in a dry, cool area out of direct sunlight.

Simply Classic Dressing

- 1/2 cup olive oil
- juice of 1/2 lemon
- 2 tbsp dried herbs of choice
- 1 tbsp prepared smooth or grainy mustard
- salt and pepper to taste

Shake in a Mason jar or whisk together to create this trés simple dressing to toss with your favourite greens.

Sundried Tomato Dressing

- 2 small zucchini, peeled and chopped
- 1 red bell pepper, seeds removed and chopped
- 2 tbsp minced sun-dried tomato
- 2 tbsp **flax oil**
- 1 tbsp dried basil
- 1 tbsp dried parsley (or 1 cup fresh, stems removed and chopped)
- juice of 1 lemon
- 1 garlic clove
- 1 tsp onion powder

Vegan Caesar Dressing

- 2 small zucchini, peeled and chopped
- 1/4 cup hemp hearts
- 1/4 cup nutritional yeast
- 2 tbsp flax oil
- juice of 1 lemon
- 1 garlic clove
- 1 tsp cumin powder
- 1 tsp **miso paste**

Soups

Soups are extraordinary in their wide variety and ability to provide many nutrients and ingredients at once. Consuming warm foods like soup during the colder months can help keep your body warm and strong, and full of veggies.

Soups prepare well in advance to freeze if you enjoy stocking your freezer with homemade, ready-to-eat meals in preparation for winter hibernation.

- Mexican Gazpacho *77*
- Miso Soup *78*
- Pearl Gazpacho *79*
- Selkies' Seafood Chowder *80*
- Turmeric Sweet Potato and Carrot Soup with Sautéed Sesame Dulse Swiss Chard *82*

Mexican Gazpacho

Serves 6

This spicy, zesty, fiesta-filled party of a gazpacho is the perfect cold soup for a hot summer day. Eating spices and hot peppers in warm weather can actually cool your body, and the addition of raw vegetables improves your hydration. Chipotle peppers have a smokey flavour that is commonly used in Mexican cuisine—we could call them an umami superstar of Mexico! They are commonly preserved and canned, though they can also be found dried in grocery stores.

- 2 avocados, diced
- 2 chipotle peppers
- 2 red bell peppers
- 1 orange bell pepper
- 1 cucumber, peeled
- 1 cup cherry tomatoes
- 1/2 cup red onion, chopped
- juice of 1 lemon
- 1 tbsp cumin powder
- 1 tbsp sugar kelp or dulse flakes
- cilantro, chopped, to taste
- sea salt and pepper, to taste
- 1/2 cup olive oil

Place all ingredients, except olive oil, in a food processor and process until smooth, drizzling olive oil as you mix.

Miso Soup

Serves 4

Traditional Japanese miso soup is made with wakame and provides a source of nourishment any time of day. In this vegan Miso Soup, we use Atlantic wakame and less cooking time in order to preserve the nutrients and flavour. Atlantic wakame has generally grown for less time in the ocean than the Pacific varieties and therefore has a milder flavour. Alternatively, you can use sugar kelp. Shitake mushrooms, which contain much umami, replace traditional bonito flakes, which are made of dried, aged, smoked tuna.

- 20 g dried Atlantic wakame
- 4 cups water
- 3 tbsp organic **miso paste**
- 1/2 cup tofu, diced small
- 1/2 cup dried shitake mushrooms (optional)
- 1 tbsp **tamari** or soy sauce
- 2 green onions, sliced

1. Bring wakame and water to a boil then reduce heat and simmer on low to medium heat for 15 minutes.
2. Remove wakame from heat and whisk in miso paste until dissolved.
3. Stir in remaining ingredients, and serve.

Pearl Gazpacho

Makes 24 mini hors d'ouevres (serves 4 as appetizer)

Perfect for your mermaid guests, this beautiful Pearl Gazpacho can be served in little canapé glasses. Garnish with toasted almonds and samphire.

- 1 tbsp olive oil
- 1 large leek, chopped
- 1 garlic clove, crushed
- 1 cup sliced almonds
- 1 English cucumber
- 1 yellow bell pepper
- 1 cup green grapes
- 1/4 cup white wine vinegar
- 1/2 cup olive oil
- 1 tsp sherry
- handful samphire, cleaned and cut into uniform 2- to 3-inch lengths, for garnish

1. Lightly sautée leek in oil over medium heat for 5 minutes or until soft and brown.
2. Add garlic and cook for another 2 to 3 minutes, taking care not to burn it.
3. Toast almonds over medium heat in a small frying pan, making sure not to burn them. They should take around 4 minutes, or until you start to smell them.
4. Put leek, garlic, almonds, and all remaining ingredients in a food processor or blender and process until smooth. You will notice the colour change to the desired milky pearl white.
5. Divide gazpacho among 24 canapé glasses and garnish with samphire.

Selkies' Seafood Chowder

Serves 4

Seafood chowder is a big deal for those of us who live by the sea. In Nova Scotia, the Chowder Trail extends from one end of the province to the other. Followers of the Trail can record their chowder experience in a little chowder booklet.

Instead of the traditional milk or cream and fish or shellfish, this vegan version uses cooked beans, which infuse the chowder with protein and other nutrients.

- 200 g cannellini, navy, or any white beans
- 2 tbsp canola oil
- 1/2 white or Spanish onion, chopped
- 3 garlic cloves, minced
- 1 carrot, peeled and chopped small
- 1 stalk celery, chopped
- 4 cups water
- 2 cups cauliflower florets
- 1 bay leaf
- 1 tbsp Atlantic wakame flakes
- 1 tsp pepper
- 1 tsp salt
- 1/2 cup nutritional yeast
- 1/4 cup dried dulse, torn into pieces
- 1 tbsp sugar kelp flakes
- $1^{1/2}$ tbsp summer savoury

1. Soak beans overnight and cook according to the directions on the package, or for rapid cooking use a pressure cooker.
2. Heat oil in a large saucepan and sautée onion, garlic, carrot, and celery over medium heat until browned and onions are translucent, about 5 minutes.
3. Add water, cauliflower florets, bay leaf, kelp flakes, pepper, salt, and cooked beans. Stir, cover, and let simmer on medium heat for 20 minutes.
4. Remove chowder from heat and let it cool.
5. Using either an immersion blender or kitchen blender, gently pulse the chowder until it is the consistency you desire. Add water if it is too thick.
6. Return chowder to stovetop and add nutritional yeast, dulse, sugar kelp, and summer savoury. Cook on medium heat for another 10 minutes, and then serve.

Turmeric Sweet Potato and Carrot Soup with Sautéed Sesame Dulse Swiss Chard

Serves 4

Dulse adds the perfect salty finish and ultimate umami experience to this puréed soup—a chilly day kind of soup that can be made in advance and frozen to stock your freezer before winter comes. Brown seaweed powder, while optional, adds depth and brings out all the other flavours, infusing the soup with trace minerals and vital nutrients.

Soup
- 1 tbsp **coconut oil** (or oil of choice)
- 1 medium sweet potato, peeled and cubed (or 2 cups butternut squash, peeled and diced)
- 5 carrots, peeled and chopped
- salt, to taste
- 1- to 2-inch chunk of ginger, minced
- 2-inch turmeric root, peeled and minced (or 1 tbsp powdered)
- 4 cups vegetable stock or water
- 1 tsp brown seaweed (kelp) powder (optional)

Sesame Dulse Swiss Chard
- 4 cups washed and sliced Swiss chard, including the stems, chopped
- 2 tsp **sesame oil**
- 2 tbsp sesame seeds
- 2 tbsp dulse flakes (or 10 g whole leaf, cut in strips)

1. Heat coconut oil, sweet potato, and carrot in stockpot over medium-high heat, sprinkle with salt, and cook for 10 minutes, stirring often or until the vegetables start to brown.
2. Add minced ginger and turmeric and cook for an additional 5 minutes.
3. Cover with stock, adding more water if needed to completely cover vegetables.
4. Boil for 10 minutes, remove from heat, let cool, and whisk in the seaweed powder.
5. Use a high-speed or immersion blender to purée the soup.
6. Place Swiss chard, sesame oil, and sesame seeds in a large pan over high heat and toss for 2 minutes. Remove from heat and stir in dulse flakes.
7. Divide soup into bowls and top with Sesame Dulse Swiss Chard mixture.

Mains

In this section, discover ocean-inspired dishes beloved by the merfolk featured in this book. Enjoy these creations with sides of your choice or on their own and discover ingredients and flavours from around the world, and close to your coastal home.

- ☆ Creamy Wakame Casserole Topped with Gomasio *85*
- ☆ DLT – The Famous Dulse, Lettuce, and Tomato Sandwich *87*
- ☆ Kelp Patties *88*
- ☆ Marinated Portobello Mushroom Burgers *90*
- ☆ Mélusine's Sea Crusted Baked Fish with Fiddleheads *92*
- ☆ Salmon Lasagna with White Sauce and Spinach *94*
- ☆ Satay Buckwheat Noodle Bowl with Seared Halibut or Tofu *96*
- ☆ Thai Mermaid Cakes with Avacado Cream or Sweet Thai Chili Sauce *98*

Creamy Wakame Casserole Topped with Gomasio

Serves 4 to 6

Long winters and cozy nights call for the humble casserole in all forms. This plant-based recipe has the feel of tuna casserole without the tuna and uses dairy-free milk and cornstarch for the cream factor without the cream. Casseroles are always a win, and they never go unnoticed at a potluck or holiday dinner.

The nutritional yeast in the gomasio recipe adds a cheesy taste with a crispy topping similar to the common northeastern tradition of using crushed crackers, bread crumbs, and even potato chips on top of casseroles, which is surprisingly tasty.

Both the nutritional yeast and wakame seaweed are noted for their range of B vitamins and can provide excellent nourishment for the plant-based diner or any human (or mermaid!).

(Continued on next page)

- olive oil
- 1/2 onion, chopped
- 3 garlic cloves, minced
- 2 cups **dairy-free milk**
- 1 tbsp cornstarch
- salt and pepper, to taste
- 2 cups broccoli florets
- 4 cups cooked pasta of choice, like fusili or a smaller, rounder pasta other than spaghetti or linguini
- 1 cup shredded Atlantic wakame
- 1/2 cup nutritional yeast
- 1/2 cup Gomasio Seasoning (see sidebar below)

1. Sauté onion and garlic in olive oil until translucent.
2. Whisk together dairy-free milk, cornstarch, salt, and pepper then add to onion mixture. Add broccoli florets and simmer for 5 minutes.
3. In a large bowl, mix together cooked pasta, broccoli and sauce, wakame, and nutritional yeast.
4. Pour into a greased 9 x 13 baking dish, top with Gomasio Seasoning, and bake at 350°F for 25 minutes or until gomasio has browned.

Gomasio Seasoning

This traditional Japanese seasoning adds a lot to any dish! Store it in the fridge for maximum freshness, and shake the bottle before using.

- 1/2 cup toasted sesame seeds
- 1/4 cup sugar kelp or dulse flakes
- 1 tsp **smoked sea salt**
- 1 tsp organic cane sugar
- 1 cup nutritional yeast

DLT – The Famous Dulse, Lettuce, and Tomato Sandwich

Makes 1 sandwich

This signature dish is featured in wondrous nooks and crannies along coastal towns of the Maritimes, most notably in the province of New Brunswick. While some humans enjoy this sandwich with bacon, mermaids often just use dulse instead and enjoy the savoury, salty, and meaty umami flavour this sea vegetable brings to the table.

- 3 slices of bread, toasted (pumpernickel, rye, sourdough, or another favourite)
- Dulse Bacon
- lettuce (whichever variety is ready to eat from the garden; spinach is another option)
- tomato, sliced
- mayonnaise (or vegan alternative)
- salt and pepper, to taste
- pickle, for garnish

Dulse Bacon

To make this salty, plant-based version of animal bacon, heat a non-stick frying pan and lightly toast dulse over a low heat until it turns crispy and brown. Alternatively, you can create a crispier "bacon" by coating the dulse in oil, placing it on a parchment-lined baking sheet, and baking it in a preheated 350°F oven for approximately 5 minutes or until the seaweed starts to bubble and brown. But be careful! Dulse Bacon burns quickly and you do not want to overcook it or it will lose its umami flavour.

Kelp Patties
Makes 12

These savoury, umami-packed, and nutritious patties are best served warm over steamed greens. Alternatively, you can make them into hors d'oeuvres or in a 9 x 9 baking dish for a loaf. The **flax meal** acts as an egg replacement and binding agent and lends a moist texture as well as healthy fats like omega-3, which is great for mermaids' skin, hair, and nails.

- 1 tbsp oil
- 1 shredded carrot
- 1 portobello mushroom, finely diced
- 1 shredded zucchini
- 2 garlic cloves, minced
- 4 tbsp **flax meal** + 4 tbsp water
- 1/2 cup oil
- 2 tbsp apple cider vinegar
- 1 tbsp maple syrup
- 1 tbsp soy sauce or **tamari**
- 1$^{1/2}$ cups **gluten-free oat flour**
- 1/2 cup nutritional yeast
- 3 tbsp sugar kelp or dulse flakes
- 3 tbsp chopped parsley
- 3 tbsp finely chopped sage (or 1 tbsp dried)
- 3 tbsp chopped thyme
- 1 tbsp chopped oregano
- 1/2 tsp pepper
- 1/2 tsp sea salt

1. Preheat oven to 350°F and line a baking sheet with parchment paper.
2. Heat 1 tbsp oil in a saucepan and lightly sauté carrot, mushroom, zucchini, and garlic.
3. In a small bowl whisk together flax meal and water, oil, vinegar, maple syrup, and soy sauce.
4. In a large bowl stir together remaining dry ingredients, herbs, and sautéed vegetables. Stir in wet ingredients and mix well.
5. Use 1/4 cup mixture to form small, flat patties and bake for 20 minutes.*

*Alternatively, to make smaller canapé-style kelp bites, use 2 tbsp of mixture, form small balls, and bake on parchment paper for 15 minutes or until golden brown. For aw full loaf size, bake for 30–35 minutes or until a toothpick inserted in the centre comes out clean.

Marinated Portobello Mushroom Burgers

Makes 4 burgers

Portobello mushrooms create a very rich, savoury barbecue winner when they are marinated and grilled. Alternatively, you can make these burgers by roasting them on a baking sheet lined with parchment paper. This recipe calls for large romaine lettuce leaves to take the place of the traditional hamburger bun for a delicioius, raw, vegan meal.

This is a great option to include at your next barbecue or any night of the week, and goes great with classic roasted potato wedges or sweet potato fries, the Mermaid-terranean Cauliflower "Couscous" (see page 103), Maritime Cauliflower Fried "Rice" (see page 101), potato salad, and oil-based coleslaw.

- 4 medium portobello mushrooms
- 1 cup olive oil + 2 tbsp
- 2 garlic cloves, minced
- 1 tsp salt
- 1 tsp pepper
- 1 yellow onion, sliced
- 8 large pieces of romaine lettuce
- 1 avocado, sliced
- tomato slices
- Dulse Bacon (see recipe for DLT, page 87)
- sauerkraut (optional)

1. Place mushroom caps in a large Ziploc bag. Whisk together 1 cup olive oil, minced garlic, salt, and pepper and pour over the mushrooms, then seal the bag. Let the mushrooms rest to marinate in the fridge, turning over once, for a total of 30 minutes. (If your mushrooms are purchased with stems, save them for a Buddha Bowl).
2. While mushrooms are marinating, heat 2 tbsp oil in a non-stick pan and start to caramelize onion on medium-low heat for 15 to 20 minutes. The trick is to not stir them too much!
3. Heat the barbecue and cook the mushrooms for 10 to 15 minutes, flipping once. (Or broil them in the oven on high for 15 minutes, flipping once.)
4. Place the grilled mushroom burger on a large romaine leaf and top with caramelized onion, avocado, sliced tomato, Dulse Bacon, sauerkraut, and/or whatever else you like!
5. Use a second romaine leaf as the top of your "bun."

Mélusine's Sea Crusted Baked Fish with Fiddleheads

Serves 1–6, depending on size of fish

The best fish options for this recipe are sustainably sourced varieties with thick skins, like mackerel, herring, trout, or sea bass. The salt will infuse the fish, and its skin will retain the moisture, making the fish surprisingly juicy. This method is commonly used in French cuisine and in the trendiest restaurants along the French Riviera.

The suggested Maritime side dish for this meal is fiddleheads, available in the spring and early summer. Be sure to soak, rinse, clean, and cook the fiddleheads well; they should never be eaten raw or undercooked.

- 3 egg whites
- 4–6 cups sea salt, depending on the size of your fish
- 1 tbsp sugar kelp or dulse flakes
- 2 tsp fennel seeds
- 1 tsp ground pepper
- cleaned whole fish such as mackerel, trout, or sea bass
- stuffing options: dulse, fresh herbs, garlic, lemon slices, sliced shallots
- 4 cups fiddleheads
- butter or oil
- salt and pepper, to taste

1. Preheat oven to 400°F. In a mixing bowl whisk egg whites and stir in sea salt, kelp flakes, fennel seeds, and ground pepper.
2. In the bottom of a glass baking dish, create a 1-inch layer using approximately half of the egg and salt mixture. Place the fish on top, stuff it if desired, and then cover completely with the remainder of the salt mix, pressing the mixture down firmly to encase the fish. Add in up to 1/4 cup water for the salt mixture to reach the consistency of damp sand.
3. Bake for 25–30 minutes or until the salt top begins to brown. The salt mixture will become firm; break it away from the fish before serving.
4. While the fish is baking, rinse the fiddleheads and soak them in cool water for twenty minutes. Bring water to boil in a medium stockpot on medium-high heat. Drain fiddleheads well, transfer to boiling water, and cook for 10 minutes. Drain well again and mix with butter or oil and salt and pepper.

Salmon Lasagna with White Sauce and Spinach

Serves 4

This style of lasagna is common in the regions of Brittany and Normandy in France, which is much like Nova Scotia with the weather, seafood, fishing, and all the sea veggies. This recipe uses smoked salmon or salmon filet, whichever you prefer, and a white sauce base instead of the traditional Italian tomato-based sauce.

- 3 tbsp butter or dairy-free alternative
- 3 shallots, minced
- 2 tbsp all-purpose flour
- 2 cups milk or **dairy-free milk**
- 1/4 cup fresh dill, chopped
- 1 tbsp sugar kelp flakes
- 1 tbsp white pepper
- 1 tsp sea salt
- 1 box (16 oz) lasagna noodles, approximately 15 sheets, cooked and drained
- 1 package (250 g) sustainably sourced smoked salmon or 2 filets (454 g) fresh salmon, cooked, skin removed
- 2 cups cooked spinach, drained well and packed
- 1 1/2 cups parmesan or asiago

1. Melt butter in a saucepan over medium heat. Cook for about 30 seconds or until browned, then add minced shallots and flour. Stir until shallots are translucent and the flour starts to brown, about 2 minutes.

2. Slowly pour in milk and whisk together. Continue to simmer over medium heat, whisking the sauce so it does not stick to the bottom of the pan. It will start to thicken. After about 5 minutes stir in dill, sugar kelp flakes, white pepper, and salt. Set aside.
3. Prepare a 9 x 13 baking pan and preheat the oven to 375°F. Lay down a layer of pasta, then a thin layer of sauce, a layer of salmon, a layer of spinach, a layer of cheese, a layer of sauce, and another layer of noodles. Repeat until you reach the top. Pour over any remaining white sauce and top with cheese.
4. Bake for 30–35 minutes or until bubbling at the edges and browned on top.

Satay Buckwheat Noodle Bowl with Seared Halibut or Tofu

Serves 2

The mermaid Satay Buckwheat Noodle Bowl has been a favourite over the years. For anyone who understands how sacred and anticipated a noodle bowl is, this is the meal for you. Goes great with grilled seafood (redfish, scallops, or haddock are alternatives to halibut) or with grilled tofu for the plant-based folk. The mushrooms and peanuts add umami, and if you want to add more sea veggies you can top the whole thing with prepared seaweed salad. For the peanut-free merperson, you can replace the peanut butter with almond butter for the same delicious and nutritious results.

- 6 cups water
- 5 dried shiitake mushrooms
- 2 portions of **buckwheat noodles**
- 1/2 cup almond or peanut butter
- 2 tbsp **tamari**
- 2 tbsp mirin or **rice vinegar**
- 1 tbsp **sesame oil**
- 1 tsp chili flakes
- 1/4 cup dry Atlantic wakame, rehydrated and roughly chopped
- handful of thinly sliced napa cabbage
- 1 tbsp oil or butter (for fish) or **coconut oil** (for tofu)
- 3 oz servings tofu or halibut
- 2 green onions, sliced diagonally
- sriracha sauce (optional)

1. Bring water to a boil, add dried mushrooms, boil for 15 minutes or until soft.
2. Add buckwheat noodles and cook for 3 to 4 minutes, being careful not to overcook.
3. Reserve 1/2 cup of cooking water, and drain the noodles using a fine mesh strainer.
4. In a saucepan, whisk together reserved cooking water, nut butter, tamari, vinegar, sesame oil, and chili flakes and gently bring to a boil over medium heat. Simmer 2–4 minutes or until slightly reduced and thickened.
5. Toss the sauce with buckwheat noodles, Atlantic wakame, and sliced cabbage and arrange in serving bowls.
6. Once the mushrooms have cooled, slice them into thin strips and place in the Buddha bowl.
7. Heat oil or butter in a wok or frying pan, sear tofu or halibut until browned on both sides, and place over noodles.
8. Garnish with sliced green onions for extra flavour and pizzazz, and add sriracha, if desired, for a spicy kick!

Thai Mermaid Cakes with Avacado Cream or Sweet Thai Chili Sauce

Makes 12 small cakes (Serves 4–6)

If you live in or have ever taken a trip to Atlantic Canada, you have surely bumped into a fish cake along the way. Fish cakes were born in the nineteenth century in the era of salt cod, when fish was preserved in salt for storing and for exporting to other countries from coastal towns like Lunenburg, Nova Scotia. Salt fish is soaked and mashed with boiled potatoes and other seasonings to create the classic Maritime fish cake. They say a restaurant's reputation is based on whether the locals think their fish cakes have the proper fish-to-potato ratio. Let's just say, fish cakes are taken very seriously around here.

Here we meet the fish cake's on-trend vegan cousin, Thai Mermaid Cakes, featuring a combination of veggies, cilantro, dulse, and Asian seasonings. Serve them with Avocado Cream or Sweet Thai Chili Sauce.

- 1 zucchini, peeled and grated
- 1 egg (or 1.5 tbsp **flax meal** mixed with 2 tbsp water)
- 1 carrot, peeled and grated
- 1/4 cup **gluten-free flour** (chickpea, rice, etc.)
- 1/2 cup toasted sesame seeds
- 1/4 cup chopped cilantro
- 1/4 cup sliced red onion
- 2 tbsp dulse flakes
- 1–2 tbsp vegetable or **coconut oil**

1. Squeeze excess water from grated zucchini and set aside.
2. Place sesame seeds in a food processor and process into a course meal. Add all remaining ingredients except oil, including zucchini, and pulse together until just combined.
3. Form small balls or flat cakes and fry in coconut oil over medium heat until golden brown and crispy. Serve with dipping sauce.

Avocado Cream

- 2 ripe avocados
- 1 tbsp coconut milk
- 1 tbsp lime juice
- 1 tbsp sriracha sauce
- salt, to taste

1. Blend all ingredients in food processor or high-speed blender until completely smooth.
2. Serve immediately and consume the same day as the avocado will turn brown quickly when it is exposed to oxygen, changing the colour and taste of the sauce.

Sweet Thai Chili Sauce

1 cup water	1 tbsp chili flakes
3/4 cup rice vinegar	1–2 garlic cloves, minced
3/4–1 cup organic cane sugar	1 tsp salt
2–4 Thai chilies	2 tsp cornstarch (optional)

1. Combine all ingredients in saucepan and bring to a boil.
2. Reduce heat and simmer 8–10 minutes or until desired consistency. You can whisk in cornstarch at the end to thicken the sauce and give it a gelled texture. Stays fresh for up to 1 week in the refrigerator.

Sides

These exotically simple sides are sure to be enjoyed on their own as a snack, as options in a buffet spread, or with your favourite protein source. Sides and are great to make on Sundays, when you can make a few different options to have on hand for lunch during the week. It's much easier to eat healthy when you have items ready to go!

Other examples of sides that are convenient to have prepared are grain salads, roasted vegetables, sliced raw vegetables, and dips like hummus.

- Maritime Cauliflower Fried "Rice" *101*
- Lemon and Garlic Sautéed Samphire *102*
- Mermaid-terranean Cauliflower "Couscous" *103*

Maritime Cauliflower Fried "Rice"

Serves 4–6

Enjoy this "fried rice" recipe raw, or fry it in a wok as is or with your choice of tofu, seafood, or meat. Fried rice can be very healthy when it includes lots of veggies and seaweed and uses tamari, and less cooking time, which preserves nutrients.

- 1 head cauliflower, cut into florets
- 2 tbsp **coconut oil**
- 2-inch chunk of ginger, minced
- 3 garlic cloves, minced
- 4 green onions, sliced diagonally
- 3 stalks celery, diced small
- 1 carrot, peeled and diced small
- 3 tbsp **tamari**
- 2 tbsp **sesame oil**
- 1 tbsp dulse flakes
- 1/4 cup corn niblets, fresh from the cob or canned
- 1/4 cup peas
- 1 tbsp maple syrup

1. Place cleaned cauliflower florets in a food processor and process until a coarse rice-like consistency. (Alternatively, use a hand grater over a cutting board.) Place cauliflower grains in a fine mesh strainer and squeeze any excess water out by pressing down with your hands. If you would like raw, uncooked cauliflower "fried rice," add all remaining ingredients except coconut oil, mix, and enjoy.

2. For cooked version, heat coconut oil in a non-stick frying pan or wok and lightly sauté the ginger and garlic for 2–3 minutes.

3. Add remaining ingredients and mix well. Continue to cook for about 10 minutes over high heat. Stir often to keep mixture from sticking to the pan.

Lemon and Garlic Sautéed Samphire

Serves 4

Samphire, also known as salicorne or crow's feet, grows in river mouths, where fresh water and sea water come together to create a unique habitat. Samphire should be sourced from a local retailer. If harvesting it from the wild, be sure to forage alongside an experienced gatherer. The samphire season in the Maritimes generally runs from late June to late August—it comes and goes quickly.

This recipe is an excellent side to serve with fish and mashed potatoes.

- 1 tbsp olive oil
- 3 garlic cloves, minced
- 4 cups **samphire**, rinsed well
- juice of 1 lemon
- salt and pepper, to taste

1. In a cast iron pan, heat oil and sauté minced garlic for 1 minute.
2. Add the samphire, lemon juice, salt, and pepper, and cook for another 5 minutes or until samphire is softened.

Mermaid-terranean Cauliflower "Couscous"

Makes approximately 6 cups

In this recipe we use cauliflower as a replacement for couscous, a wheat-based product that many people think is a whole grain but is essentially very small pieces of pasta. Cauliflower couscous is a perfect gluten-free option, also suitable for anyone looking to incorporate more whole foods into their diet. Fresh cauliflower also contains more water content and fibre than traditional couscous, so you will feel full longer and get more water at the same time.

This is a great dish to make the night before and have ready to go for your lunch. While it is very filling on its own for a snack, it pairs well with seared fish or tofu, Mermaid Thai Cakes, grilled mushrooms, or alongside a large garden salad. Stays fresh for up to 3 days in the refrigerator.

Fun Fact

Aphrodite, the Greek goddess of fertility, was born from sea foam and was also worshipped as goddess of the sea. She originates from from Cyprus in the Mediterranean region.

- 4 cups cauliflower couscous* (1 medium cauliflower)
- 1/2 cup dried Hana Tsunomata, rehydrated**
- juice of 1 lemon (about 1/4 cup)
- 1/4 cup orange juice
- 2 tbsp olive oil
- 1 cup cucumber, diced into 1/4-inch pieces
- 1 orange bell pepper, diced into 1/4-inch pieces
- 1/4 cup minced red onion
- 1/4 cup sliced scallions
- 1/4 cup chopped mint
- 1/4 cup chopped parsley
- salt and pepper, to taste
- optional: chopped Thai chili peppers, ground cumin powder, avocado, or cilantro

Cauliflower Couscous: To create small, couscous-like pieces, use a hand or box grater; chop using a food processor; or place cauliflower florets in a blender filled with water to cover the florets. If using blender method, blend on high speed for 5 seconds and strain well.

****Seaweed preparation:*** Place dried Hana Tsunomata in a glass bowl and cover with room temperature water. Let sit 10 minutes, strain, pat dry, and roughly chop before adding to the couscous.

1. Whisk together the liquid ingredients and add to Cauliflower Couscous.
2. Mix in vegetables and let marinate for a minimum of 30 minutes so all of the flavours come together.

Desserts

It is true that most mermaids have a sweet tooth. Here you will find a treasured selection of plant-based desserts that not only satisfy a mermaid's cravings but offer a way to consume more glow-enhancing ingredients.

While some of these recipes have seaweed or spirulina as optional ingredients, you can add them to most desserts and baked foods to enrich them with nutrients or to add fluffiness to breads and muffins.

- ☆ Carrot Bunny Cake with Ocean Frosting *107*
- ☆ Mélusine's Classic Mermaid Pie *109*
- ☆ Micro Fudge Truffles *111*
- ☆ Raw Chocolate Mousse *112*
- ☆ Raw Kiwi Coconut Lime Tart *113*

Carrot Bunny Cake with Ocean Frosting

Serves 4–6

Ah, carrot cake! A cake of memories, a cake of spice and carrot wonder. This recipe uses a variety of flours to create the ultimate gluten-free and dairy-free carrot cake. Sorghum and buckwheat are ancient grains and have an earthy taste and higher density than white cake flour; the brown rice flour adds density and also binds the cake together. Applesauce can be substituted for oil if you would like a lower-fat version.

Note that the cashews required for Ocean Frosting need to soak for 2 hours beforehand, so you should set them to soak before you make the recipe, or you can make the frosting ahead of time; it stores well in the refrigerator for up to 3 days.

- 4 cups carrots, peeled and shredded (5 or 6 large carrots)
- 1 cup organic cane sugar
- 1 cup vegetable oil or applesauce
- 1 egg
- 1 ½ cups sorghum flour
- 1/2 cup brown rice flour
- 1/2 cup buckwheat flour
- 2 tsp baking powder
- 2 tsp cinnamon
- 1 tsp baking soda
- 3/4 tsp ground nutmeg
- 1/4 tsp ground clove
- 1 tsp kelp powder or 1 tbsp sugar kelp flakes (optional)

1. Preheat the oven to 350°F.
2. Mix together carrots, sugar, and wet ingredients in a large mixing bowl.
3. In a separate bowl whisk together dry ingredients, then add to the carrot mixture. The mixture will be heavy and solid but should be moist.
4. Grease a baking sheet with coconut oil. Spread mixture evenly onto the baking sheet and pierce it all over with a fork.
5. Bake for 25–30 minutes, or until a fork comes out clean.
6. While the cake is baking, prepare Ocean Frosting.
7. Let cake completely cool on a rack, then remove from pan and cut into four sections. Lay the first piece on a serving plate or platter. Start to ice the cake, spreading a layer of frosting evenly on top. Add the next piece and layer with icing. Repeat for third and fourth pieces, then ice the sides of the cake.

Ocean Frosting

- 1 cup cashews, soaked 2 hours, rinsed, and drained
- 4 tbsp maple syrup
- 1 tbsp fresh lemon juice
- 2 tsp **spirulina** powder
- 1/2 tsp vanilla extract

Place ingredients in a food processor and process until smooth.

Mélusine's Classic Mermaid Pie

Serves 4–6

This recipe is a vegan spin on the blancmange dessert that is known in many countries in different variations and dates back to medieval times, when it was often given to sick people for healing when it wasn't being served as a delicious dessert.

Mélusine made quite a few of these in her time, on those Saturdays she took for herself. This version uses mermaid favourites maple syrup and dairy-free milk. We must also recognize the Acadians—who came to the Maritimes from France and were responsible for much agricultural and fisheries growth—in their use and interpretations of blancmange and their ability to utilize the ingredients around them here in l'Acadie, notably Irish moss.

Mélusine's Classic Mermaid Pie is extra delicious when served with blueberry, raspberry, rhubarb, or strawberry compote.

Filling
- 15 g dried pink Hana Tsunomata or wild Irish moss
- 1/2 cup almond milk
- 1/2 cup maple syrup
- 3 tbsp **coconut oil**, melted
- 1 tsp orange, lemon, or lime zest

Crust
- 1 cup pitted dates
- 1 cup dried cashews or pecans
- 1 cup shredded coconut
- 1/2 tsp cinnamon

1. Soak Hana Tsunomata or wild Irish Moss for 15 minutes in cool water.
2. Combine all filling ingredients in a stockpot over medium heat then reduce heat to low and simmer for 20 minutes.
3. Pour mixture into a bowl through a fine mesh sieve and set aside.
4. Using a food processor, pulse together dates and nut of choice into a course meal. Add shredded coconut and cinnamon and pulse together.
5. Sprinkle the base of a 9 x 9 springform cake pan with additional shredded coconut and press in the crust mixture.
6. Pour filling mixture over top and refrigerate for a minimum of 20 minutes until the dessert is firm before serving.

Micro Fudge Truffles

Makes 12

Do you have a sweet tooth? Most mermaids do. These fudgey, raw, vegan, gluten-free truffles are infused with spirulina micro-algae and packed with fibre. Their bite-sized convenience makes them easy to carry around in a food container in your shark's purse, in the fridge for an anytime dessert, or stored in your freezer. Micro Fudge Truffles are dense and chewy thanks to the dates, maple syrup, and walnuts.

- 1 cup dates, pitted
- 1/2 cup walnuts
- 3 tbsp maple syrup
- 1 tbsp sugar kelp or dulse flakes, or 1 tsp spirulina
- 1 tsp pure vanilla
- 1/4 cup cocoa powder + 2 tbsp

1. Add all ingredients except the additional 2 tbsp cocoa powder into a food processor and process on high for about two minutes or until the mixture has started to combine.
2. Add 2 tbsp cocoa powder to a dry bowl, and then start forming the truffles into balls.
3. Place the formed truffles into the dry cocoa bowl to coat, and then place on a parchment-lined air-tight container before refrigerating.
4. It is best to keep these in the fridge—although they won't last long!—and they freeze well.

MERMAID RECIPES

Raw Chocolate Mousse

Serves 4–6

Avocados have a lot to write home about, including their healthy fats and creamy texture. After 20 minutes in the fridge, this mousse will firm up just like the traditional French version. It has been this mermaid's number one recipe to test on her mer-friends who are unsure about vegan foods. They often cannot tell that there are sneaky avocados in there.

Eat within a day—but that should not be too difficult!

- 4 ripe avocados
- 3/4 cup cocoa powder
- 3/4 cup maple syrup
- 1 tbsp melted **coconut oil**
- 1/4 tsp sea salt
- optional extract/flavour/seaweed additions: cherry, dulse flakes (1 tbsp), mint, orange, **spirulina** (1 tsp), or sugar kelp (1 tbsp)

1. Place all ingredients in a high-speed blender or food processor and process until smooth.

Raw Kiwi Coconut Lime Tart

Serves 4–6

Refreshing, sweetly satisfying, and perfectly good for you, this dessert uses three limes. It might remind you of key lime pie. We use pecans as the nut of choice in the raw crust recipe, and the pie filling is made firm by the use of fatty coconut milk and coconut oil.

Crust
- 1 cup shredded, unsweetened coconut
- 1 cup dates, packed
- 1 cup pecans

Filling
- 6 kiwis, peeled
- 1 banana
- 1/2 cup coconut milk
- juice of 3 limes
- zest of 1 lime
- 2 tbsp **coconut oil**
- 1 tsp **spirulina**

Topping
- kiwi slices
- strawberry slices
- toasted coconut
- lime zest

MERMAID RECIPES

1. Begin by making the crust, combining all ingredients in a food processor.
2. Press the crust into the bottom and up the sides of a 9-inch spring-form pan, pressing down evenly in the centre. Store the crust in the refrigerator until the filling is ready.
3. Combine all filling ingredients in a high-speed blender until the mixture is completely smooth.
4. Pour filling into the prepared crust and place in the refrigerator for a minimum of 30 minutes to firm up before serving. You can also fast-track this process by cooling it in the freezer and serving it as a frozen dessert.
5. To decorate, alternate sliced kiwi and strawberry, completely covering the tart. Sprinkle with toasted coconut and lime zest.

Mermaid Hair and Body

This is the section that we have all been waiting for! If you spend as much time in the bathtub as the average merperson, you are always on the lookout for new ideas. Our bodies love natural ingredients and so many products to make the recipes in this section can be found right in our kitchen cupboards.

- Blonde Hair Rinse *117*
- Coconut Sea Hair Mask *118*
- Deluxe Whole Leaf Kelp Soak *119*
- Fairy Dust for the Bath *120*
- Mermaid Bath Salts *121*

Blonde Hair Rinse

Has your blonde hair gotten a bit dull or lost its lustre? A bit too much sun or not enough? Try this quick natural boost to blonde hair and add shine to your mermaid mane. Pasteurized apple cider vinegar will work okay, but raw apple cider vinegar will give the best outcome.

- 1/4 cup raw apple cider vinegar
- 1/4 cup lemon juice

1. Stir the apple cider vinegar and lemon juice together.
2. Shampoo your hair as normal, rinse, and pat dry, and then apply the hair rinse throughout your locks right over the top of your head, being careful to avoid your facial skin.
3. Rinse with warm water and follow with your regular conditioning routine. (Don't worry about the smell—the shine will make up for it.)

Note: Be mindful if you are going in the sun afterwards to first thoroughly rinse any vinegar or lemon juice that may have gotten on your skin.

Coconut Sea Hair Mask

This mask is a great way to prepare your hair for a day at the beach or swimming in the ocean. Alternatively, it can be used at home whenever your salty hair feels like it needs a moisture burst. If you do not use the full amount, you can store the mask in your fridge for up to 1 week. (If using the mask on your skin, be sure not to spend too much time in the sun after applying.)

- 1/4 cup virgin **coconut oil**
- 2 tbsp brown seaweed powder
- 2 drops mint **essential oil**

1. Mix all ingredients together.
2. Comb mask through your hair, then wrap hair in a warm towel or securely using a scrunchie and leave on for up to 30 minutes.
3. When it is time to rinse out your mask, select your shampoo of choice and follow your regular shampooing routine. (As your hair will already be divinely moisturized, you do not need to use conditioner afterwards.)

Note: Please be mindful when rinsing the mask out of your hair to ensure that oil is not left in the tub afterwards!

Deluxe Whole Leaf Kelp Soak

As we know, bathing is an important ritual for any merperson. This allows us to retreat to the comforts of our watery home when we are visiting land. It's a place to go to for rejuvenation. Therapeutic baths have been enjoyed around the world for centuries and by many civilizations.

Soaking in a tub full of kelp is an Irish tradition. In Ireland there are bathhouses where you can lie like a mer-queen amidst the healing treasures that seaweed has to offer, including skin softening and clarifying. It might also ease a stubborn cold or winter ailment.

When the kelp meets steamy warm water it releases compounds that turn to gel—be sure to have a cold rinse afterwards, and try to prevent the kelp from going down the drain.

- 2 lbs fresh rockweed or sugar kelp (ask your local seaweed producer where to find the purest source)
- a few drops of your favourite **essential oil**

1. Rinse the seaweed and refrigerate until ready to use (within 24 hours of purchase).
2. Add seaweed and essential oil to a steamy bath, and soak.
3. Rinse yourself in cold water.

Fairy Dust for the Bath

Makes 2 3/4 cups

There is always a time and place to use a sprinkle of Fairy Dust in the bathtub. Store Fairy Dust in an airtight container to keep the magic fresh.

- 1 cup Epsom salt
- 3/4 cup baking soda
- 1/2 cup sea salt
- 1/3 cup citric acid powder
- 3 tbsp kelp powder
- 10 drops **essential oil** of choice (see next page for some mermaid favourites)

1. Mix all dry ingredients together well in a large mixing bowl, and then sprinkle the essential oil droplets over top, and mix again.
2. Sprinkle a pinch of Fairy Dust in your bath, cast your spell, soak, and enjoy!
3. Store remaining Fairy Dust immediately to retain the scent.

Mermaid Bath Salts

Makes approx. 5 cups

Salt baths are relaxing and good for the body because their natural minerals can be absorbed. If you are sensitive to essential oils, you can use herbal tea instead, like mint or chamomile.

Many mermaids reportedly take at least one bath a day, if not more, and that does not include trips to the ocean, lake, or river. Adding Epsom salts and seaweed powder is a way to harness the powers of nature in your bathtub for those times when you cannot make it to the real ocean.

- 1 kg Epsom salts
- 1/2 cup dried brown seaweed powder
- **essential oil** of your choice (mermaid top picks: cedar, eucalyptus, jasmine, lavender, lemon, mint, patchouli, rose, tea tree, thyme, vetiver)

1. Mix together all ingredients in a large bowl.
2. Sprinkle a handful of Mermaid Bath Salts into a hot bath.
3. Store remaining Bath Salts in Mason jars or non-plastic containers.

For Our Furry Friends

In the ocean, mermaids' best friends are seals, which are not unlike furry puppies and dogs that humans keep as pets. When mermaids are on land, it is only natural that they love dogs and all the other land creatures.

Dogs generally love seaweed. Maybe it's the salty taste, or maybe dogs just know what is good for them. Treat your favourite furry friends to these dog treats!

- Beach-Dog Snacks *123*
- Doggy Treats *125*

Beach-Dog Snacks

Makes about 2 dozen strips

These tasty treats are sure to delight your canine friend on any special occasion. The recipe calls for a food dehydrator; however, if you do not have one at home, you can bake them by spreading evenly onto a parchment-lined baking sheet, pre-heating the oven to 375°F and baking for 20 minutes. Remove from the oven and cool before storing in the refrigerator. You can also freeze.

- 1.5 lbs salmon filets
- sea salt (for seasoning)
- 3 tbsp **flax meal**
- 1 tbsp dulse flakes
- 1 tbsp pea protein powder (plant-based protein source available in many health food aisles)

1. Preheat oven to 425°F.
2. Place salmon skin-down on a parchment-lined baking sheet and season with sea salt.
3. Bake for 10 minutes, turn the filets over, and continue cooking for another 8 minutes.
4. Remove salmon from oven and let rest for 5 minutes.
5. Place the cooked salmon, skin, and cooking juices into a high-speed blender and process until smooth.
6. Add flax meal, dulse flakes, and pea protein and pulse together.

7. Pour onto a food dehydrator sheet (or sheets, depending on the shape and size of your dehydrator).
8. Spread the mixture evenly, approximately 1/3-inch thick, and then cut into long strips or bite-sized pieces with a butter knife.
9. Dehydrate for minimum 12 hours, and then serve to your fur-friends!

Doggy Treats

Makes approximately 60 small treats

These salty dog treats are nutritious and tasty, and something every mermaid should keep handy! They will stay fresh for up to 2 weeks in the fridge and freeze well.

- 1 cup **gluten-free flour**
- 1/2 cup instant oats
- 2 tbsp dulse, wakame, or kelp flakes
- 2 tsp baking powder
- $1^{1/2}$ cups cooked mashed sweet potato
- 1 cup raw grated carrot
- 1/2 cup organic peanut butter
- 2 tbsp water

1. Preheat the oven to 375°F.
2. In a large mixing bowl combine flour, oats, seaweed flakes, and baking powder, and then form a **well**.
3. In a separate bowl, combine all remaining ingredients, mixing well, and add to the well in the dry mixture.
4. Combine wet and dry ingredients then form the dough into a ball. Roll out on a floured surface to 1/4 inch thickness.
5. Use a cookie cutter to shape the treats, then place them on a parchment-lined baking sheet and bake for 20 minutes. Cool before serving.

A Mermaid's Glossary

bivalve: The common name to describe mollusk species, and other water-dwelling creatures that have a hinged shell and lack a backbone, such as clams, scallops, oysters, and mussels. A mollusk has two (bi) valves that help it move around, and to open and close its shell.

buckwheat noodles: These noodles are very flavourful and also soak up the delicious flavours of whatever food they're topped with, making them the perfect base for your choice of protein. Just be sure not to overcook!

coconut oil: A great option for sautéeing and cooking, coconut oil is also used for the beauty products featured here. This oil is commonly used in raw foods for its ability to become firm when cooled.

dairy-free milks: These include almond, coconut, oat, rice, soy, and sunflower in unsweetened or flavoured varieties. You can also make them easily at home by soaking the nuts or seeds to unleash their active benefits and then processing them in a high-speed blender.

essential oils: Strong potions that are extracted from plants and flowers and have different healing and aromatherapy benefits. The essence and medical compounds of the species are reduced down to a concentrate that can be purchased at many health and grocery stores. When selecting your essential oils for food and beauty creations, be sure that you are choosing natural essential oils and not perfumed or scented oils.

flax meal: Ground flax seeds provide many nutritional highlights. They are used in vegan, raw, and gluten-free baking as a plant-based egg alternative for their ability to bind ingredients (make them stick together). It is best to purchase whole flax seeds first then grind them as needed at home.

flax oil: This is a nutty, flavourful, and highly nutritious oil when used in cold recipes like salad dressings. Rich in omegas and other essential fatty acids, this oil and other cold-pressed oils should be stored in the fridge once opened and kept out of direct sunlight to preserve their nutrients.

gluten-free flours: Most gluten-free flours, including sorghum and brown rice, are available at health-food stores, bulk-food stores, and the natural-food section of grocery stores. Oats can also be ground in a high-speed blender to create a nutritious gluten-free flour.

Herbamare: This unique product invented by a Swiss herbalist is produced mainly in France and found in most grocery stores. Herbs and kelp are infused with sea salt, producing incredible flavour, which means reduced salt intake. Even if you're not following a low-sodium diet, you can simply enjoy Herbamare for its fantastic taste.

hoisin sauce: A delicious Chinese condiment traditionally made with fermented soybeans, and has a deep barbecue flavour. It is somewhat sweet and is slightly saltier and thicker than Teriyaki sauce. It is often eaten with fish, meats, or drizzled over noodle and rice bowls.

intertidal zone: Beaches may look simple, but there are layers of the tide that make up the complex and intricate system of aquatic life at the shoreline. The intertidal zone describes the area of the beach that is exposed to air (oxygen) at low tide, and then covered again at high tide. The intertidal zone consists of the low, high, middle, and upper tidal zone which all appear at different times during the day.

miso paste: A Japanese condiment made by fermenting soybeans and the fungus kōji with salt, and sometime ingredients such as seaweed or rice. It is used in marinades and sauces, and is essential to miso soup.

natural sugars: Dates, coconut palm sugar, and maple syrup are all natural alternatives to white and brown sugars or agave nectar, which in general should be avoided.

photosynthesize: The verb (action) of the term "photosynthesis," which is the biological process for how plants, algae, and some bacteria turn energy from the sunlight into food. Plants take in the heat of the sun, and through a chemical process, convert sugars and other nutrients into energy. So very simply, it is how plants eat to gain their energy and grow.

pigments: Naturally occurring compounds in plants that can be extracted to create the ingredients we use for colouring things like face creams, foods, and even Easter egg dyes. Pigments can be found in things like carrots (beta-carotene; orange), or trees (chlorophyll; green) for example.

polysaccharide: A type of carbohydrate that exists in certain plant species which can be removed and used commercially in the textile, health-care, food, and industrial manufacturing industries. A neat example is fruit pectin: in fruit, this substance helps keep the walls of cells joined together, but if removed, it can be used to thicken jams and other sweet confections.

rice noodles: These gluten-free noodles come in various shapes, including vermicelli or thicker pad Thai noodles, and are sometimes found in brown rice or spinach varieties. They make a great addition to rice paper wraps.

rice vinegar: Rice vinegar has a sweet flavour and should be used in moderation. It is a key component of sushi rice. It can be found in the international section or in Asian grocery stores.

samphire: A salty aquatic plant that is found growing in river mouths generally in the months of July and August. It can typically be found seasonally at supermarkets and fresh grocers in coastal regions of the UK, Eastern Canada, and France. It is also known as "crow's feet" or "salicorne."

sesame oil: Toasted sesame oil will give the most flavour and can be used while cooking but should not be used to fry with because it burns easily. The cold-pressed version has a different flavour and should be eaten only in cold recipes, like salad dressings.

smoked sea salt: Salt is the enhancer of all flavours, and smoking it adds incredible depth and flavour, or Umami, to dishes. To make smoked sea salt, the salt is smoked for a period of time using apple wood, oak, mesquite, or hickory wood, infusing it with a smokey flavour. It can be purchased at most grocery and health-food stores.

spirulina: This interesting superfood is an incredible source of iron and protein and is actually a blue-green microalgae. It is cultivated in lakes or growing systems in warm subtropical regions. In addition to being nutritious, spirulina has a beautiful green colour that can be used to naturally colour icings and other dishes.

tamari: This fermented soy sauce with deep umami flavour is the liquid that floats to the top of tempeh, a fermented soybean product similar to tofu but using whole soybeans pressed together. The Japanese equivalent to Chinese soy sauce, tamari can be found in the international section of most grocery stores.

well: To "form a well" is a term used to describe when you take the ingredients that have been mixed together in a dry bowl and form a hole in the centre of the bowl. Once the well is created, you pour wet mixtures into it and begin to stir together. The point of the well is to properly mix the wet and dry ingredients together to desired consistency.